Michael Myers Shoemaker

Trans-Caspia

The Sealed Provinces of the Czar

Michael Myers Shoemaker

Trans-Caspia
The Sealed Provinces of the Czar

ISBN/EAN: 9783337417239

Printed in Europe, USA, Canada, Australia, Japan

Cover: Foto ©Andreas Hilbeck / pixelio.de

More available books at **www.hansebooks.com**

TRANS-CASPIA

THE SEALED PROVINCES OF THE CZAR

BY

M. M. Shoemaker

Author of " Eastward to the Land of the Morning;" "The Kingdom of
'The White Woman''

✳

CINCINNATI
THE ROBERT CLARKE COMPANY
1895

PREFACE.

As I send these notes of last summer's journey out into the world for better or for worse, he whose protection we enjoyed for many months lies silent and cold in death within the cathedral fortress of Peter and Paul.

From our entrance into his dominions at Wirballen to our departure at Irkeshtan the power and protection of the Czar were forever around us, and though at times it seemed to one from America irksome to be so eternally watched, yet I could not but feel with it all a sense of security utterly impossible under any other power. The face of Alexander III., as it smiled down upon us at every point or post, through the Caucasus and Georgia, over the Caspian Sea and Black Desert, at Bokhara the Noble and fair Samarkand, at Tashkend and Osh, or in some lonely outpost of the "Valley of Paradise," was forever that of a friend.

The mere mention of the name of the "Little Father" insured us protection in city or hamlet, on the steppes or the mountains; and when I wandered back from the deserts of Western China, sick and weary, his painted semblance banished a world of trouble. The journey was long and full of interest, amongst people and cities but little known to our western world. I venture, therefore, to hope that these notes may afford, to those whose travels must be by books alone, some small portion of the pleasure that my wanderings have given to me.

M. M. S.

CINCINNATI, *December* 25, 1894.

CONTENTS.

—

(vii)

Contents.

TRANS-CASPIA:

THE SEALED PROVINCES OF THE CZAR.

CHAPTER I.

> Dost thou see on the rampart's hight
> That wreath of mist, in the light
> Of the midnight moon? O, hist!
> It is not a wreath of mist;
> It is the Czar, the White Czar
> Batyushka! Gosudar!

BERLIN, May, 1894.

SECURING the proper document this morning at the consulate of our country, I proceeded therewith to that of his Majesty, the Czar, in order to assure my entrance at Wirballen into Holy Russia. I had fully expected—as of old—to be closely questioned as to whether or no I was a Jew—whether my parents were Jews, and if so, why so—but the fact that my passport already bore the visá of the Russian

consul in New York caused its representative
here to arise and salute most profoundly, assuring me that Holy Russia was as an open book
to me, and strongly hinting that our consul here
knew these facts when he made out my docu-
ments; knew them when he demanded my fee—
16 marks; also suggesting that I return and demand restitution.   However, knowing that our
consul-general was at the time lying dead,
poor man, and that his " understudies " had done
their best, I pocketed my loss and moved on to
the frontier.   There are two of us,"and we are
bound for the ridge-pole of the roof of the
world," the distant and gigantic Himalayas.   It
is our intention—Russia and England consent-
ing—to pass, *via* Samarkand and Osh, to Gilgit, in Cashmere.   The way is long, and may
be hot and may be cold, but we shall go forward.
I carry with me letters from the Marquis of
Ripon to the Viceroy of India, and am assured,
also, of all the assistance I desire when I reach
St. Petersburg.   De B. has gone forward, and I
must take the long ride to that city alone; therefore, I decide for a two nights' journey instead

of two days. I can always sleep in a train, and the way is deadly uninteresting. Though passport restrictions are very great in Russia, I can not but feel that I am well taken care of, and that it would be impossible to "disappear" unless the authorities desired it. I am also impressed with the knowledge that, if they so desired, my disappearance would be most complete—"gone" would be an excellent epitaph, after which it would be well to place an interrogation mark. On setting out on a tour like this in Central Asia, one can not but wonder what the end will be. If you have ever gazed upon the Himalayas, you will understand what it means to penetrate those solitudes, and the place toward which we are moving is *beyond* those solitudes. The "Pamirs." Our route lies over the Caucasus and Caspian Sea—through Merve and Bokhara to Samarkand, and thence into the wilderness of plains and mountains to the southeast, until the mountains be past and the roses of Cashmere breathe us a welcome.

"Guide Abbas available for two months and perhaps longer by arrangement." That is the answer to our telegram sent from the chief city of Holy Russia to the English consul at Odessa. Abbas is a guide of experience, such as we will need to pilot us through the vast solitudes of the Pamirs and on downward into Cashmere. We wire him to hold himself in readiness to move at a moment's notice, though according to the usual slowness of Russian officials Abbas will have to possess his soul in patience for some days at least. Russia is not anxious to have even such disinterested persons as a Dutchman and an American penetrate into those lands of great and constant debate between herself and the English Lion. However, we mean to go, and have therefore moved on the powers that be with all the collected artillery of the Holland and American legations and embassies, both here, in England, and in Holland. I am sorry to say that my own government appeared, until I reached our embassy at London, both ignorant and helpless. The honorable secretary of state insisted upon it that no extra passport was necessary, and I truly believe that such names as Samarkand, Osh, Merve, Bokhara, Gilgit, Tashkend, and Kashgar, conveyed no meaning to his mind. So, aside from the visá of the Russian consul at New York, my passport left our country without indorsement. Our ambassador in London fully understood all the difficulties and rendered me most useful assistance by procuring letters to the Viceroy of India from those high in authority in her majesty's government, securing a passport from the Chinese minister, and in many other ways. Our minister here in Russia had already put the wheels in motion, and I found on arriving that every thing would be granted—at least that is the hope and belief at present; and as B. has received every necessary permit, there is no reason to imagine that I shall be refused. At any rate, we have telegraphed Abbas to meet us at Tiflis, while we shall go by rail to Vladikavkas, some seventy-six hours to the southward—no very charming prospect. There we shall take stage over the mountains of the Caucasus to Tiflis. That will be something grand! From Tiflis we take the train—seventeen more hours—to Baku, where

we cross the Caspian.   But let us leave further
"itinerary" for the present.

We look forward to pleasant weather over the
Dariel Pass, as the spring here in Russia is a
month ahead of its usual time.   The changes of
the seasons are very rapid in this land of the
north.   To-day is, at noon, warm and balmy,
and yet but three weeks back snow lay thick on
the "Islands"—St. Petersburg's great pleasure
park, around which flows the majestic Neva, and
on one side of which the delicate spire of the
Cathedral of Peter and Paul rises from the
center of the terrible fortress prison of that
name.   Under its shadow sleep the royal dead
of Russia from Peter down to Alexander II.
As we sit in the legation to-day, discussing
coffee and cigars with Mr. White, a brilliant
sun lights up the gold on the delicate spire of
the royal sepulcher, the green woods of the
"Islands" and dancing waters of this grand
river, shines over a scene of most entrancing
beauty—so beautiful that one forgets that those
low red walls surround the suffering living
dead as well as the silent emperors.   Those

walls of Peter and Paul encompass and entomb
more horrors than the Bastille ever did, and together with that other prison, the *Schlüsselburg*,
some two hours away on the banks of Lake
Ladoga, constitute Russia's greatest fortresses.
To them the poor wretches are carried first, and
on any, and sometimes every, night while we are
sleeping, the midnight requisitions are going on,
separating dear ones, plunging them forever in
those great bastions, only to pass thence to the
grave, or worse than the grave—the mines of far
Siberia.

Some of the members of the diplomatic circle
claim that Russia is charming—in fact, the most
charming place in Europe for those of their rank
to live in. One man, from Switzerland, whose
duties are over, avows his intention of living
here the remainder of his life. That is as it may
be. Of course, I can not contradict him; but
when I ask of the " people," he shrugs his
shoulders and claims that they are too debased,
too ignorant, and too stupid to care for advancement, too sodden to be able to use greater
privileges if granted unto them. A century or

so may change this; but now, knowing not of their own misery, they have no desire for, nor could they utilize, any greater freedom. "And what of those who have reduced them to this?" "One must not criticize the Czar." The people must not praise him, for that would imply a right to blame him. The people must say nothing and do nothing, otherwise the *Schlüsselburg*, Peter and Paul, the mines, and Siberia, death having long since ceased to be a terror in Russia. Yet it struck me upon my entrance at Wirballan on Saturday, that the espionage and restrictions were not nearly so great as a few years since. My luggage was scarcely examined at all, and I noticed that it was likewise with crowds of the most suspicious-looking characters. I could have smuggled no end of Nihilist litera-ture and other contraband articles, and perhaps the very fact that less attention is paid to such things makes their authors less anxious to introduce them. A constitution for Russia was signed by the late Czar, and was to have been promulgated in April, but his murder on the 1st of March, 1881, ended all that. Anarchists, Nihilists, and their like will never succeed until they acknowledge that no good ever comes from evil. Alexander was a noble, progressive ruler, and the people in Russia murdered their own cause when they blew him to atoms. Poor man! He rests over there in Peter and Paul near his broken-hearted father, the great Emperor Nicholas; while not far off Catherine sleeps, dreaming somewhat of her little German home, but more often of her many lovers. On the tomb of the late Czar, Dolgorouke keeps fresh flowers always, but his wife, the lonely Empress, is remembered by none.

Apropos of this same Empress, there is a story told by the guides of St. Petersburg—all idle talk, perhaps, and almost too sad to repeat. She was, as the world knows, a victim of consumption, and had been exiled to Italy by her physicians; but her homesickness became so great that she prayed hourly to be allowed to return to Russia. Finally the Czar asked if it were possible, and was told that, if a suite of apartments could be arranged so that the temperature would stand always as it did in Italy, she might be taken home and might live there for some months. So it was done. Rooms in the "Winter Palace" were provided with triple windows to keep out the cold, and the sufferer was taken back. For a little while she was happy, and then the terrible disease, stayed apparently for a season, asserted itself, and her sufferings became so great that her prayers for death drove the Emperor to inquire how long she would live if the cold were allowed to enter. "Twenty minutes," was the reply; and the cold was allowed to enter, and she died "in twenty minutes," "utterly alone"—so the story runs. The old guide babbled on as we wandered from room to room of the vast pile, now into the golden drawing-room, now into the vast white throne-room, near which is that strange bust of the great Peter. Finally he led us into a small apartment, furnished like a soldier's tent, while every here and there lay folded handkerchiefs, on which I read in faded ink the name "Nicholas." The garrulous old custodian droned on and on, telling a story of how the great Emperor, broken-hearted over the Crimean War, had one day summoned to his presence an obscure chemist of the city, and commanded him to " furnish the Czar with a potion that would end life quickly and painlessly." At first the man refused absolutely, but he was told that the " Czar " commanded it, and his life would be the forfeit of a refusal. So it was given, and the chemist, guaranteed safety, was conducted over the border into Germany, where he shortly was found "dead in his bed;" but in the meantime " Nicholas " had been found dead, here on this simple cot before us. Truth or fiction, I know not, but such is the story. There is no fiction, however, about that other terrible bed in the room below it, where Alexander the Second was laid after the explosion in 1881, and there he died, and the traveler of to-day shrinks with shuddering away from the blood-stained mattresses. The gorgeous fêtes and splendid court functions pass away and are forgotten, but these " shadows " forever abide amidst the gloomy splendors of the Winter Palace.

Funeral ceremonies are something terrible in this Greek Church. They buried on Friday last a grand duchess. The diplomatic corps were summoned at 10, and from 11 A. M. until 2 P. M., all, from the Emperor to the lowest, stood on the cold floors of Peter and Paul. One strong soldier near the catafalque grew suddenly white and rolled over. The Czar himself, and he only, retired for an hour. No one ever sits in a Russian church, so you can fancy the fatigue. It is, however, a great sight to go, for instance, to St. Isaac's, which to my mind is the grandest church in Europe, and see the thousands of worshipers, the large majority of whom are men, standing or kneeling in silent prayer. I notice that the people crowd up around the priests, seeming to take actual part in the conducting of the services. Off to one side a choir of magnificent voices roll out grand music, for no tone save that of the human voice—God's instrument—ever awakens the echoes of a Russian church. The shadows were very thick in St. Isaac's yesterday. Long rifts of sunshine lit up here and there some jeweled shrine or malachite column. Tapers glimmered faintly before the numerous Icons. Gold and silver, marble, bronze, and lapis lazuli, glowed faintly or slumbered in darkness. The air was heavy with the odor of incense, while over the thousands prostrate in prayer, one deep grand voice breathed a benediction: " Peace be unto you ; peace be unto you." Verily one could almost fancy that peace had come unto Russia, until, turning, they caught through an open doorway a glimpse of the distant " Peter and Paul."

St. Petersburg is a grand city as to distances and general effect. Her river is superb, her squares immense, her churches and monuments surpass any in Europe ; but the architecture of her houses and palaces strikes me as most inferior. The Winter Palace is simply immense, but neither grand nor beautiful inside or out. The " Hermitage " presents a notable exception, and is certainly a very pleasing structure, while its portico stands unrivaled in Europe. The caryatides thereon are colossal, and were carved,

I believe, by an uneducated Finn. If so, he could give lessons to most of his craft on this globe. I do not know their equal. But, however, as this is to be a journal of Asia, I will say no more about this city of the North.

CHAPTER II.

May 22d.

I HAD a sample of Russian red tape and slowness to-day. My application for permission to pass the Pamirs went in on Saturday last. This is Tuesday. Yesterday was fête day, Sunday ditto, to-morrow ditto. I went this morning, with our military attaché—a very nice fellow, by the way—to General ———, to see whether the permission could not be hurried somewhat, as the weather here is nasty and we want to get into the sunshine, of which we will probably have more than enough before we reach the Vale of Roses. General ——— was only approached after much formality and the passing in review of many aide-de-camps. However, we reached him at last—reached him in his inner sanctum, surrounded by numerous war maps of this terrible empire, conspicuous among which were those of Turkistan and the Pamirs. Of course, Russia absolutely controls all that section, and the desired permit could be given in five minutes and with few strokes of the pen. Yet this comfortable official looked us calmly in the eyes, knowing that he was delivering himself of nonsense, and knowing that we were fully aware of that fact, and assured us that the minister of war would be most happy to ask the Governor-General of Turkistan for our permission, but that it must be done by numerous telegrams to that distant region, all of which would take some days, and they had only been at work on it " four." He would be happy to do all he could, but we must await the pleasure of those rulers of the Far East.* So we bowed deeply and departed.

I know of no more dreary place for tourists than St. Petersburg in bad weather, when the rain is coming down in torrents. After one has done the sights of the town, there is nothing for it but to retire to one's hotel, which is far from good, but good as Russian hotels go. I was told by a foreign secretary, whom I met at

* The Governor-General at Tashkend, the Ameer of Bokhara, the Governor of Askerbad, and the Governor of Osh.

dinner last night, that it was for strangers in winter most desolate. If you do not possess your own home and do not care for society, you are dreary, indeed. The "Islands" are, of course, closed, most of the bridges over the Neva being taken away until the ice goes out in April. There are but few cafés in the town. The Opera and French theater form the stock of play-houses, to get into either of which you must be "booked" weeks ahead. Day commences at 11 A. M. and ends at 2 P. M., when darkness and the snows come down over Russia. The rich who live here make life gay, but God keep the poor! One can not but contrast these wretched peoples with the happy, free-from-care darkies of our Southern States. There is never any music or banjo playing here. One never sees a dancing bear surrounded by dancing people. It is all sodden wretchedness for the poor of Russia.

The authorities have delivered their ultimatum as to an Englishman whom we still had hopes of getting through. They will not allow him to go under any circumstances. We had hoped that he might be allowed to pass as a servant or secretary; but no, it must be given up, and to-day's mail carries two letters to London that will make him blue as indigo. It would have been an excellent thing for one in his position, an officer, to make the tour; and then again, he must be back at his Indian post in August, and must now go *via* the oft-traveled route of the Red Sea. I am warned by the authorities to be careful and state upon every occasion that I am an American; and to-day I spent an hour plodding the streets in a pouring rain in a vain search for an American flag, and very odd it seemed not to be able to find that of which every child at home has dozens.

Desiring to secure the visá of the Chinese minister, I sent my passport there to-day, only to have it returned with the information that the entire embassy had gone for a several days' picnic to Finland. To-morrow will be another fête day, during which nothing will be done, but we shall move southward on Thursday, and wait on the other side of the Caucasus at Tiflis, which, by the way, means "warm spring." Even if one misses the Pamirs, the Caucasus is well worth a journey of seventy-four hours by railway to see, although a railway journey in Russia is flat, stale, and most unprofitable.

May 25th.

News came last night from our legation that Russia had granted my pass, but the same messenger brought her final refusal to pass B., of England. A telegram came from London that my Chinese passport was also en route. So we start to-morrow, and it rests now only with myself and the good God as to whether I go beyond Tiflis. We owe much to the kindness of Prince G., who has given us several letters and introductions that will prove of inestimable service, not the least being that to his guide and servant near Osh, whose services he has placed at our disposal, stipulating only that we return him from Bombay to Prince G.'s estate in Odessa, and not allow him to go to America, that Mecca of all the world.* Prince G. has made the tour both ways, and, knowing the route, has given us a tracer. We learn that near Hunza Naga, to the north of Gilgit, we

* On reaching Margeland, we discovered that the man was in jail for robbing his master.

may have some trouble. Therefore I purchase another revolver, with which I have not the slightest doubt I shall do myself more harm than the enemy.

There is quite a discussion on between De B. and myself concerning the time necessary to make the passage from Osh to Gilgit. Prince G. says "one month," De B. two and a half. The latter would bring our arrival about November 1st, or long after the snows had set in on the mountains. If such is the case, I do not make the trip. We are not explorers, and can not give the world any information it does not already possess. That being the case, I am not disposed to risk a winter on the Himalayas. On my part, this is supposed to be a pleasure tour, and I do not think that could be called, by the most enthusiastic traveler, "pleasure." It will take us some time to get up our train of ponies, etc., at Samarcand, and we must make a detour to Tashkend to visit the governor-general, some two hundred miles of a detour. But it must be done. De B. dotes on governor-generals, maharajas, and their kind.

CHAPTER III.

EN ROUTE, June 25th.

ST. PETERSBURG, with its rain and mists, its stately churches, and its plaster palaces, has vanished. Moscow, in all its oriental gorgeousness, is on view from our railway carriage. The gold domes of St. Savior's, surrounded by the many belfries of the Kremlin, and the vast spread of the city, all red, green, and blue, seems to float in a sea of emeralds. The view is something like that over Delhi, yet how different! Yonder is Sparrow Hill, from which Napoleon first saw the city, and just below one catches a glimpse of the nunnery where Peter the Great shut up his sister. As we passed from one station to the other this morning, we encountered one of those sad bands of prisoners so common in Russia—two women and a man, from whose faces all hope had long since died out. They were bound to far Siberia, a journey as long as ours.   We are also going by "order of the Czar," but how different the modes of travel !   Guarded by five soldiers, they passed on with downcast heads, while we, attended by the same number of obsequious porters, went merrily by them.   They did not even look at us, and their world paid no attention to them. "Only some of the poor, and there are many such."   This is ancient Russia, ruled aforetimes by that suitor of the good Queen Bess of England, "Ivan the Terrible."   He sleeps under one of those domes yonder, where daily thousands of his subjects kiss his forehead, a spot of which is shown through a hole in his coffin.

The winters are not quite so terrible here as in St. Petersburg, and the pine trees are losing a little of that sad droop, telling of the heavy snows that bend them downward through so many months.   As I awakened this morning, the sun was just rising from behind a forest of thick pines, whose waving branches across his red disk looked like the tails of many wolves. One is glad to be behind wooden walls, for it is never quite certain there may not be wolves around at any time. Indeed, in winter they penetrate to the suburbs of the greater cities, and render it unsafe to be out alone in any village of the empire.

This land is the native spot for the lily of the valley. At every station we are bombarded by boys carrying high baskets of the lovely flowers, and we are told that they grow luxuriantly all up and down the Volga. It will take us forty hours to make the journey from Moscow to Rostoff, but we are comfortably settled in a compartment, which we bid fair to keep to ourselves, so we shall not mind it greatly, and will be amply repaid for the hours spent therein if we only have fine weather for the passage of the Caucasus. Strange that those lilies should be here! One associates them with France and the sunny South, not with frozen Russia. Yet here they are, and one bright-faced boy tosses a huge bunch in at our window as the train moves off.

As I gaze over these vast plains of the empire, I can not but wonder where all the millions of her people are keeping themselves. The towns and villages appear to have many more buildings than are necessary. Few people are seen at the stations, few seen over the boundless green floor that stretches away to the horizon, broken by scraggy trees and now and then by green balloon-domed churches. The land seems rich, and under a progressive rule should blossom like the rose, but what incentive have these people to make more than will keep body and soul together. We shall cover some twelve hundred miles, a small fraction of the empire, between the Capital and Rostoff, near the Sea of Azov, all under the absolute rule of one man, trembling for his life in his guarded palace at Gatchine, forced by fate into a position terrible to think of, into an existence certainly not much better worth the living than are those of the wretchedly poor throughout his dominions. While in addition he is held personally responsible for every act of cruelty throughout all his vast empire. Acts that he knows not of and is powerless to prevent.

Our third day southward brings a change. The air has suddenly become balmy and spring-like, and the grass is of a tender green. Over the boundless floor dash companies of horsemen—Cossacks. The country resembles portions of the Holy Land. Suddenly, as if by magic, five lofty mountains spring into view, and there, away to the right, like a pile of clouds, rises Mt. Elburz, Europe's grandest mountain, whose peak soars four thousand feet higher than Mt. Blanc. From this point it rises solitary and alone from the plains, because of the distance, which so far render its companions invisible. Here the watering places begin, the one we are coming to being guaranteed to make good and sound all diseased livers, and solve Mallock's problem. This is the great granary of Europe. In fact, the soil of the entire empire looks rich enough to provide food for all the world, if only her people were encouraged to cultivate it to its full capacity. The country grows more pleasing as we approach the mountains, while the air comes ladened with the perfume of the acacia tree, whose white blossoms brush our carriage windows as we move onward. I am

MT. ELBURZ—4,000 FEET HIGHER THAN MT. BLANC.

interrupted by the porter. His intense desire to keep every atom of dust out of this car makes us rather uncomfortable. These Europeans, outside of England, have absolutely no idea of real cleanliness or true sanitary arrangements. Here is a new and very handsome car, with roomy adjustable chairs, which make it a very pleasant sitting-room. At one end are three or four state-rooms, all one could wish for. But there all semblance of comfort or even decency ceases, and one comes to the lavatories, etc., etc. The former possess a faucet from which water will flow only when you hold it tightly, and when it does come it squirts up your sleeve, over your head, down your back—any place, in fact, save in the basin, which, by the way, is purposely so arranged that the fluid immediately runs out. The closet is simply vile, and it never enters the head of the porter to in any way cleanse it, although he will spend an hour on one window which shows outside. So it is in all hotels. France, Germany, and Italy in the larger cities have much improved of late years, but as for the

rest the less said about it the better. One
ceases to wonder that cholera has an abiding
place at all seasons in these countries.

Vladikavkas, "This side of the Caucasus,"
but to my mind very far the other side of all
the rest of the world, is a wide-streeted, sunny
town, overtowered by gigantic mountains and
surrounded by running streams and green
meadows; wretched hotels where not one word
of any thing save Russian is spoken or understood. It is only after several trials that we
succeed in obtaining rooms for the night at a
hotel whose name I do not know and shall not
ask. We finally discover a man who speaks
German, and he is instantly dispatched to the
diligence office to pay for our seats to Tiflis.
They had been secured by telegraph from
Moscow, but because we did not appear within
half an hour of the arrival of our train, 11 P. M.,
they have been given to others, and we are
forced , either to remain another twenty-four
hours here, or go to the expense of a separate
conveyance. This last is decided upon, and

with strict orders to have it ready at 7 A. M., we depart to seek a little rest.

Seven A. M. brings a man who calmly informs us that the horses can not be ready until ten o'clock. No use swearing, though I am afraid we did. One can not but think that stage and hotel are in connivance to detain us here and to force the separate conveyance, which is, of course, much more expensive (50 roubles against 25), upon us. Perhaps they have also had time to inform their friends the banditti on the mountains. At any rate we hunt up our revolvers, and I discover, after conspicuously displaying mine and sending off my trunks, that the thing is not loaded, and my ammunition is for the day quite beyond my reach, all of which, I doubt not, is an interposition of Divine Providence in our favor, our danger being greater with than without fire-arms. This is always so at such times. Those who may attack us are of course better armed, and would fire on our first movement, life being nothing to them; whereas, otherwise, I fancy they would simply rob us. Russian inspection is a blessing on this tour, as our every step is followed, and we ean not "disappear." It is known at all times just where we are and are going, and our arrival at the next point is looked for; hence a delay here of six hours even would send the forces of the empire in search. So it will be in Turkistan. We are not given a passport or any sort of credentials to that land, but simply notified that we are permitted to travel therein, the notification coming in the shape of an informal note to our legation, and we have been asked by what route we desire to move. Within twenty-four hours of the granting of the permission every point in that vast and lonely land, lonely to us because of our isolation amongst thousands of natives, has been advised and is looking for our coming. Therefore, when one travels the unbeaten paths of farther Asia, it is well to go with the benediction and under the eye of the Czar.

Ten o'clock finds us en route for Tiflis. Our carriage, an ordinary victoria, being loaded with luggage of all sorts and of the most non-

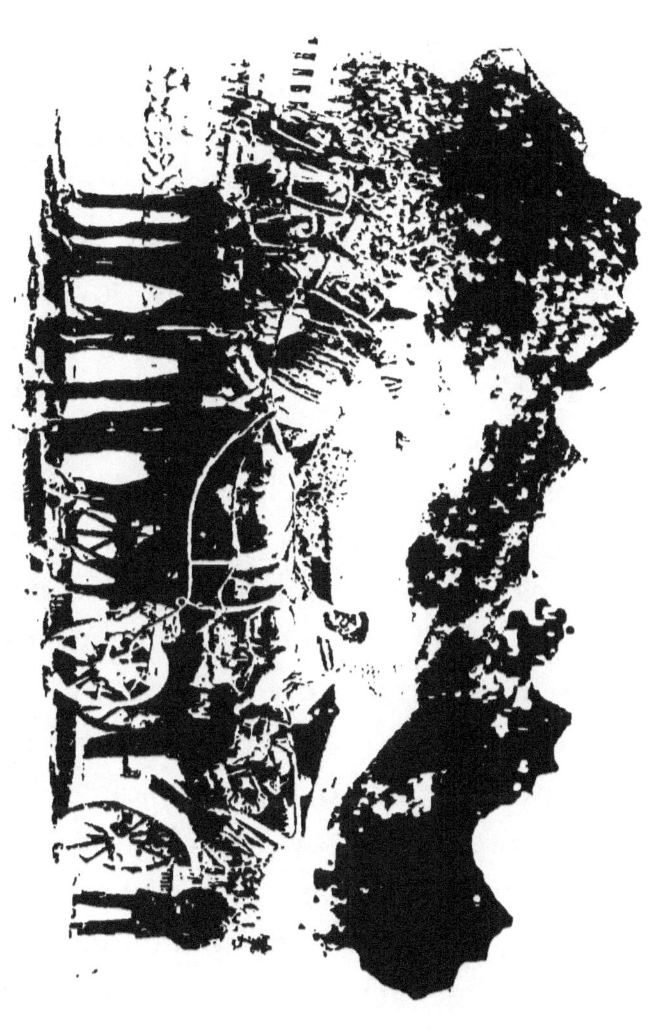

descript kind.   Two huge rolls contain our beds
and bedding, four tin boxes our perishable
"togs" (one must have a dress coat even in the
Pamirs), two large kodaks, a rifle, a shot-gun,
four   revolvers,   numerous   hand-bags,   Indian
hats, etc.   De B. thinks so much of his tin
boxes that he has had them incased in wood, the
result being that they look like baby coffins, and
our arrest for infanticide has been imminent
several times.   Mine are plain tin boxes, painted
black, the " U. S. A." thereon having caused
me to be most profoundly saluted by all the
officers met with.   However, all is at last tucked
away, and we are off to the mountains, bowled
along at a rapid rate by four horses abreast.
Every ten versts they are changed, so that a
smart trot, or, more often, a rapid gallop, is kept
up all day long, though we ascend to some
seven thousand feet.

The Caucasus are beautiful, and rise like a
vast triangle, with the perpendicular toward
Europe.   Therefore the view from the north is
much grander than from the south.   Prominent
from amongst the great snow peaks soars,

CONE OF THE KASBEC.

second only to Elburz, which I spoke of yesterday, the glittering cone of the Kasbec, where the tortured Prometheus hung quivering. We pass it to-day about 4 P. M., as we rattle along over the superbly built military road, which our country holds nothing of its kind to equal. All along the pass rise towers, and in many instances whole castles and towns, all in ruins now, showing the work of the robbers of old; and not so very old either, as this road ten years back was not safe, nor can we rest assured that we will not be robbed of our luggage even now. It happened not long since to the Governor of Tiflis, who, en route to greet the Czar at Vladikavkas, had his entire luggage stolen from the back of his carriage without being aware thereof until he reached his destination.

This is the only portion of Europe where I have found absolutely no English, French, German, or Italian spoken. Nothing save Russian; and when you are presented with a bill of fare it is " Greek " indeed, that language, as you know, using the Greek letters. These hotels are of the most primitive sort. You are charged extra

THE CASTLE OF QUEEN TAMARA.

for towels, though they do furnish you with a small amount of water.

Snow peaks rise around you in bewildering confusion on this Dariel Pass, and you drive through miles of snow before you reach the summit. The scenery reminds one of that of the Engadine and the Stelvio, though I do not think the mountain of the Kasbec quite equals the " Ortler Spitz," and all other mountains are as nothing when once one has gazed on Kinchin-jinga from Darjeeling. However, the Caucasus have a beauty peculiarly their own, and every peak and crag, every tower and castle, is covered with some legend of robbery and murder in the old, free Georgian days. That is all over now, and your aforetime robber drives your coach most dextrously. They are a fine-looking race, these drivers, very dark and stalwart. Our last driver to-day was the very picture of " Darius the King," as one sees him in the carvings from Babylon—tall and majestic, his fine dark face and jet-black curly hair and beard surmounted by one of these huge peaked turbans of Astra-kan, his figure robed in the ulster-like garment common to his people, while his boots would have done justice to Bond street. We rather hesitated to offer him the usual fee when we changed him. Twenty kopeks (ten cents) did seem small payment to this Assyrian monarch. He evidently thought so, too, for he swore at us. It is dark again ere we reach where we put up for the night, leaving sixty miles more for to-morrow.

The first signs that the manners and customs of Asia were being gradually neared were at Vladikavkas, where an ordinary Brussels rug was nailed up on the wall as a thing of beauty. Here, on the top of the range, the rugs are of inferior workmanship, but are Turkish work; and as I look from my window on arising, I am convinced, by a lot of camels quietly browsing near by, that this is Asia, and not Switzerland. A few notes of barbaric music clash into sound and sink into silence, and the dogs have that wolfish look so common to those of the Far East. From here onward until we descend into India, we shall have to do with tribes, and not nations, save where the leaven of Russia and

England affects the whole. I trust that the protection of those nations may preserve us both, if not for our own sakes, at least for some of those at home. We know that these Caucasians are superb riders, and yet if we were to attempt to ride so at home the result would be disastrous. The knees are very much drawn up, so much so that only the very tip of a pointed shoe touches the stirrup-iron, and often not even that. These horses keep up a constant dancing motion, which would dismount us with but such a hold on their backs. But these men seem to be perched securely, and manage to carry a gun or two, with several pistols and dirks strung around their belts. Cartridges are arranged across their breasts on their dark coats, the skirts of which, spreading out far back over their horses, produce, with the animals' flowing manes and tails, a sweeping, graceful, but rather funereal effect.

Our second day's journey is entirely down the southern slope of the mountains, where the scenery loses nearly all its ruggedness, and becomes almost as " pastoral " as our Alleghanies.

Not patriotic, that, but true. Our eastern hills do seem almost pasture lands by comparison with the stupendous cliffs of Asia. The day's ride is very beautiful, and as we fortunately have slight showers, there is no dust, while the air is ladened with all the delicious fresh odors of spring. A Vermont boy would be amused at the attempts of these people toward tilling the soil. The plow used is of the most primitive description, and is drawn by ten yoke of young steers, guarded and conducted by seven men. The field that they are at work upon certainly is not more than three acres in extent, and at their rate of progress it should be ready for planting about October 1st, this being only May. The Vermont boy, with a good plow and stout pair of horses, would do the whole thing between the hours of milking and his noonday dinner, even allowing time for the removal of the usual rocks to be found on all New England farms. Numerous ruined castles and towers are passed, perched high up on the mountains or close to the rushing river. The religion of the people has changed to Mohammedan, and all Russian

churches are now inclosed in high, strong,
fortress-like walls; otherwise such jewels as
adorn their shrines would prove too tempting
to the followers of the Prophet.

Down at last into the valley of Tiflis! To our
amazement, the heat is not great, and the valley
reminds us of many in France. Hedges of

RUSSIAN CHURCH AND FORTRESS IN THE CAUCASUS.

primrose, poppies, and corn flowers, roses and
cherries; yet with all its resemblance to France,
there is a certain indescribable something that
recalls the "Land of the Vulture," and we
should not be surprised to see the minarets of
Cairo rise from the valley before us. The
resemblance is even stronger when Tiflis comes
in sight. The ancient capital of Georgia looks

very eastern, very oriental, in the evening sun-light. But the first entrance into her streets convinces us that we are still under the dominion of the Czar. Russian police stand here, there, and every-where, and the wide berth that is given them demonstrates better than words the control that government exercises over this southern possession. There is a monument near the western entrance of the town, on the spot where the Czar Paul nearly lost his life through a runaway team. It would not have been a bad thing if the accident had succeeded in ridding Russia of that licentious monarch. I fancy that the Empress Catherine imported her "particular friends" from this section. The men are very handsome, but of the far-famed Georgian women I can say very little. From here the Turks of old procured their beauties, and the types which pleased them are still plentiful in the streets of Tiflis—huge in size, flabby, chalky skins, faces with no ray of feeling or intelligence. That was their idea of beauty, and they could not have come to a better market.

CHAPTER IV.

TIFLIS.

IT is a vast comfort after the inferior hotels of Russia—inferior not so much in the structure as in the management—to land at the very clean and delightful Hotel De Londres here. Mine host and his mother are Germans; hence the cleanliness. It gives one a homelike feeling to be so welcomed, convinces one that after all the traveler "finds his warmest welcome in an inn." How that quotation recalls the splendors of the Ponce de Leon, and the senseless, useless life one leads therein. But let us come back six thousand miles or more to Tiflis, the last few miles of which have been very dusty and we descend from our carriage a sight to behold, and in no very good humor. Cross? Yes, somewhat! Even I have been known to be cross now and then. Nor is my temper—our tempers I should say on this occasion—improved by having a porter drop our medicine chest and smash several bottles therein, thereby soaking the whole with their contents. However, the accident is not without its good side, as the broken bottles contained cholera mixture, so no matter what we take it will contain something useful for our perhaps unknown disease. We can not, therefore, go far wrong in the administration of drugs. B. knows absolutely nothing about drugs. I am somewhat better informed, through sad experiences, so that unless I am insensible I can keep an eye on him, otherwise he would be apt to administer flea powder for a cold, give me a bath in pure ammonia, or perhaps recklessly administer all the contents of the case at once.

How dirty we are, how delicious the huge baths of the town feel to our tired bodies. The water is naturally hot and I sit for half an hour under a strong spout. There is absolutely nothing that they will not furnish you at these bath houses, if you pay for it. But all things are very expensive at Tiflis, as I discover this morning when I desire to cable home—six roubles per word ($3.00); more than from Calcutta. I know it is wrong, pure robbery, in fact, but I must send the cable. As the rates from London are only one shilling per word to New York, all the rest, with the exception of our inland rate at home, goes to the lines between here and England, or to the operator's pocket here, which is much more likely. I think from B.'s actions last night that he must have partaken of some of the mixed contents of that medicine chest—flea powder, I fear.

By the way, concerning the ride from Vladikavkas to Tiflis, I would recommend every one to take a carriage. It costs more, fifty-two roubles, but will amply repay. The stage is always slow and most wearisome. The one we missed, and which started three hours before us, reached here four hours after we did. There are but three good seats, all in the second class. The arrivals at the stations are very late and the departures correspondingly early, and you will be worn out, whereas we traveled at a rapid pace and had all the horses we wanted at every station; never less than four. He who travels in his own conveyances is, in all lands and especially here, an English "Milord." The stage even, as it does not carry the mails, gives place to him, and at his disposal are the best rooms and horses. The mail goes in a separate well-guarded conveyance, traveling night and day.

As is the case with so much in the East, Tiflis does not bear close inspection. It is picturesque from a distance and its situation is beautiful, but the town in its interior is neither one nor the other, and there is not an interesting mosque or building in the place. Its bazaars are common-place, and, like most bazaars, dirty—but not picturesque in their dirt. In addition they are absolutely wanting in all that peculiar charm which makes those of Cairo and Tunis so delightful to wander through and linger in; nor does one find here displayed all the thousands of attractive articles which in those other cities cause him to return ladened to his hotel. Through the center of

TIFLIS.

the town between deep walls of rock, down
which pours the sewage of the place, sweeps
the river, as repulsive looking a stream as I
have ever seen.   This hotel is an oasis amongst
eastern hotels and renders Tiflis bearable; otherwise the three days I am forced to spend here
would hang heavy on my hands, though I
pass much time in wandering alone through
the town.   Fortunately it is a cool season;
one could not desire more magnificent weather
than that of yesterday and to-day.

Abbas, the guide, arrived from Odessa this
morning.   He is better than I expected, and
has crossed the Pamirs several times, as well as
other out-of-the-way routes in Asia.   I sincerely
hope he will turn out well.   Littledale, the
traveler, gives him a good reputation, though he
does say that the man is lazy.   His ideas as to
time are mixed, to say the least.   This morning
he told me that it would take us until December
1st to reach Cashmere, and an hour later that
the 15th of September would see us in India.
We shall see what we shall see.

B. insists that I do not do justice to Tiflis.

He knows nothing of the other oriental cities—
hence his feelings, which are deep, very deep.
I might have described this river and the cliffs
as possessed of the beauty of Eden, but it would
have been somewhat wide of the truth; I might
have filled these bazaars with old silver, antique
fire-arms and swords, and fairy stuffs of all
sorts; ladened their air with the perfume of the
roses and lilies; made you drink delicious coffee
and eat " Turkish delight" therein, while you
stared at the veiled women and gorgeously
costumed eunuchs; I might have described a
mosque that would surpass that of " Sultan
Hassan." But I fear, had you come here and
found the river and its cliffs repulsive, the bazaars full of all that is unattractive, the coffee
and Turkish delight entirely lacking, ditto the
mosque, you might have voted me a fraud. It
will surely be better to find this capital of the
Georgians better than you had expected, and
if you pass her by, contenting yourself with
the panorama she displays, you will vote her
enchanting; for the world, I think, holds no
more superb view than that presented by

this city of Tiflis approached from the great Dariel Pass over the Caucasus.

The Queen Tamara—she of fame and romance—reigned in rose-ladened Tiflis some eight hundred years ago. She was wise as she was beautiful, and during her time the city reached its greatest height of prosperity. Then, all the known arts and sciences flourished in this ancient kingdom; but after her death, "Tchinghiz Khan"* swept like a black cloud over the valley, leaving such desolation and destruction that Tiflis has never recovered her ancient glory.

I met this morning in the court of the hotel an Englishman, who has been living here for five years—at least he has lived in the country that length of time; and when I questioned him as to the climate, he replied that to those who lived here hell possessed no further terrors, that is, in the matter of heat. We certainly have been most fortunate. It is quite cool to-day, the rain having refreshed every thing. Trees of any size are unknown in Georgia. I noticed

* Hereafter I shall use the simpler form of that name.

QUEEN TAMARA.

in crossing the Caucasus that nothing larger than a scrub was to be seen: no forests of stately pines near the summits, no dense groves of majestic trees lower down, no "isles of the forest" spreading around one; plenty of green, but all so diminutive that even the telegraph wires are supported on rails from the railroad, to which are bound sticks of timber certainly not more than ten feet long, but quite as long as can be found here, or anywhere around here. The result is that refuse petroleum is the usual fuel.

To-morrow we start for Baku, from which Russia draws those vast stores of that fluid which enables her to rival our "Standard oil." Baku is on the Caspian, and there we certainly should find it hot, the level of that inland sea being some eighty-five feet lower than the Black.

The *Standard* of the 22d arrived from London this morning with almost one-third of its principal page blotted out by the authorities. I wonder how long Russia expects that such childish treatment of people in this nineteenth century will be allowed to continue. Surely, a nation whose actions will not stand the light of day through a free press is in a strange position, and yet her people submit, and have long ceased to care for what may go on in the outside world.

Abbas has just returned from an errand of mine concerning some lotion for the hair, for which I had given him the prescription. One of the ingredients is *cantharides.* These chemists refused to make it up without a Russian doctor's prescription, and sent me word that "I might want to poison some one."

TIFLIS, June 2, 1894.

I am awakened this morning by a burst of martial music, and find that the town is all alive with soldiers. It does not take long for a traveler to don his clothes, and I am soon in the public square, toward which the military are wending their way from all directions. At its entrance stands a small Russian church, and the music of the many bands becomes reverential and tender as they pass the holy Icons, although

their selections are somewhat singular, " Ta ra
ra boom da ah " being most conspicuous. I
confess to being somewhat shocked, and almost look to see one particular saint in a long
purple garment strike into a skirt dance.   But

no ; neither does he drift into a waltz as the
tender notes of "Auf Weidersehen" are wafted
on the air. This is the anniversary of the day
when Russia finally settled, in the conquest of
Schamyl, the Caucasus question, in which she
employed 180,000 men to conquer the 15,000
of that robber chieftain. Chief of Daghestan
was Schamyl, and as Russia has obliterated that

country, its very whereabouts will soon be forgotten. It included these mountains and the land to the north-east thereof as far as the mouth of the Volga. Schamyl was taken first to St. Petersburg, and then allowed to retire to Mecca, Russia knowing that the holy well in that city would finish him off, as it very promptly did, and has done for so many thousands. To-day his conquerors celebrate all this by holding high mass in the gardens here. The soldiers are arranged in a huge square, and stand at attention as the general passes around in inspection. Suddenly he stops and stares with apparent horror, and one fancies, not only by his expression, but by the anxiety depicted on the faces of his staff, that at least a plot against the entire empire has been unearthed. I confess I laughed aloud when I saw one of the staff rush forward and straighten the white cap of a soldier, it having become cocked over his left eye as he was " presenting arms," so that he could not arrange it himself. I fancy that he will spend the night in the guard-house, and I know the empire must shake to its base with such a terrible matter.

Russia does not neglect the religious welfare of her troops. Daily attendance at mass is required, and to-day her priests, gorgeous in green and gold and purple, hold high celebration of the sacred rite. Then one and all are blessed, and with a fanfare of trumpets the troops move off to their barracks, and we retire to pack up, as we leave at noon for Baku.

CHAPTER V.

RAILROADS here are conducted in a somewhat unusual manner. It is always necessary to go to the station at least half an hour
before the time of starting, and even then you
will be hurried at the last. I fear Abbas is little
better, if any, than old Thomas, my Indian
servant. At least, he completely loses his wits
in the station at Tiflis, and I am forced literally
to shake him once or twice as he insists upon
running after every one's luggage save ours.
The confusion is enormous, and "worse con-
founded" every moment, while the waiting-
rooms look like a city camping out. We are
just one hour getting booked and seated, having
had in that time the usual number of rows with
people who tried to impose upon us. Settled at
last, Abbas informs us with an injured air that
he has no seat. That is a little too much. We
have waited on him, though we pay for the

contrary. Now he may stand if he can not get seated. We tell him so promptly and he departs. A white-haired, pleasant-faced old gentleman enters our compartment with his arms ladened with roses, of which he presents us with a handful. His smiles and his flowers come like a rift of sunshine through the clouds.

I am told that this company is systematically robbed by its employees. It is a constant occurrence for the conductors to waylay people as they approach the booking office. After assuring them it is unnecessary to purchase tickets, he hustles them into the cars. For a rouble or so, which, of course, the company never receives, they travel as far as they like. All goes well unless an inspector happens to board the train and demand a look at the tickets. Then the dead-beats without them are hustled onto the roofs of the cars and told to "lay low." This happened not long since, but, unfortunately for the conspirators, one of the road guards, seeing the roof travelers, imagined that something was wrong, and flagged the train. The sudden stoppage rolled the wretches pell-mell to the ground, broken legs, arms, and many bruises being the result. That stopped the nefarious traffic for a time, but it is in full swing once more.

I should like to send these notes home as I write them, but I fear they would not be allowed to pass through the mails, though I have said comparatively little about subjects that have been so exhaustively treated by other travelers. Russia is very sore over what has been written, and does not mean to permit any more such works if she can prevent it. But can she prevent it? People from afar will come to Russia and will exercise that freedom of speech to which they have been born. Therefore, so long as they write the truth, Russia must expect much from their pens that will not meet with her approval. Those who come from progressive nations to this absolute monarchy of the Middle Ages must be struck with surprise and horror at the state of affairs here displayed. Dazzled they will be by the splendor of the rich, and horrified by the condition of the people; and so it will be, and will be written of, until the empire throws off her chains and swings into line with progressive Europe. I was asked yesterday whether I did not see a great resemblance between the "Steppes" and our western plains. Yes, certainly, so far as the part which nature has to play; but over those western plains the very winds seem to sweep ladened with life and hope and progress, while the faces of our people are happy and contented; but here, the resignation of despair throws a mantle of hopelessness over empire and people. With no future, no past, these millions rise with the sun, toil under its passage, and go to bed when it does, having no hope or desire save to eat and sleep. They will not awaken to help themselves, because they do not know that they are badly off; and so it is policy to keep them ignorant, lest with greater enlightenment other desires might come not consistent in an empire, where seventy millions must bow to the will and caprices of the few who rule. Therefore, the students are kept at Latin and Greek, lest they yearn for forbidden fruit. But it can not last, this being the nineteenth century.

Order is evolved out of the confusion, and we get under way on time, only to be delayed an hour just outside of Tiflis. This entire valley between the two seas seems constantly windswept. To-day it almost blows a hurricane. The country is not tropical, possessing much such a climate as Ohio, until the greater heat comes, later on. At Akstafa one is on holy ground, that being the station for Ararat. Over this valley drifted the ark, and into this valley descended the inhabitants thereof. Mt. Ararat rears its snowy crest one hundred versts (seventy-five miles) to the southward. It is believed by the natives to be haunted by Genii. No man has ever ascended it, so *they* say, though the contrary is well known. The overland telegraph from London to Teheran leaves us here and starts south-eastward across the mountains; but the easiest road to that city of the Shah is *via* Baku, and thence by boat to the southern end of the Caspian, where you commence a three days' journey overland and directly southward.

Abbas has wonderful tales to relate concerning his prowess with the wild men of the moun-

MOUNT ARARAT.

tains, amongst whom we are to pass. Perhaps it is all true, but one certainly has little to fear from any thing, man or beast, that could be intimidated by Abbas. I think we shall get an extra guide in Samarkand. Huge trains of oil tanks pass us constantly, showing our approach to that great source of Russia's wealth. The night turns cold and the winds rise almost to a tempest. When morning comes, we are running along the shores of the Caspian, which, strange to say, after the commotion of the elements last night, is as placid and peaceful as a mill pond in August.

CHAPTER VI.

BAKU, June 3, 1894.

OIL, oil, every-where! in the gutters, in the mud of the streets, in the food one eats, and in the air one breathes! It would also be in the milk one drinks, but for the fact that it has been boiled out. "We dare not drink raw milk here." Even the dogs, cats, and hogs running wild in the streets are streaked with the grease that oozes out of the pores of the earth. In places it spouts forth in such quantities and with such force that it has never been possible to utilize the entire production of Mother Earth. The great structures, or "Blacktown," as the localities are called, are a mile or so out of the city, and loom darkly on the horizon—as one approaches from Tiflis—a mass of towers, scaffolding, and dense black smoke. We have just returned from a visit to one of them (having seen one you have seen them all), and for half

BLACKTOWN.

an hour use our utmost endeavors to shake or brush off the fine, oily, and yellow powder with which our clothes are saturated. There is little satisfaction, save to one particularly interested, in visits to such places—huge masses of machinery, vast lakes of oil, grease and dirt saturating every thing. Here and there is a spouting oil fountain, almost equal to "Old Faithful," in our Yellowstone Park. Over all hangs the dense pall of smoke. How the people manage to live is hard to understand. Baku proper consists of an old Tartar town surrounded by a still perfect wall, which is something more than nine hundred years of age. Inside thereof we found the usual picturesque tangle of houses and mosques. Turbaned men and veiled women, Astrakans, Turks, Kirghiz, Turkistans, Daghestans, Persians, Russians, dogs, dirt, one American, and one Dutchman crowded the streets. With our departure, the latter nations lost their representatives in the ancient capital. Dirt is here, dirt is there, dirt is every-where; and one would not enjoy it in the least were it otherwise.

OIL WELL.

We are, for a time, much disheartened to learn that three Americans, Robinson, Thurston, and Watterman, who desired to enter Turkistan, have been turned back from Usin-ada. I had heard of them in our legation at St. Petersburg. It seems that they had been waiting at Batoum for the necessary permit, which had been telegraphed them. But they had nothing to show at Usin-ada save Mr. White's telegram, which the authorities refused to honor. Therefore, they have recrossed the Caspian and are now en route to Ararat. The question arises as to whether we are much better off. We hold personal letters from the authorities in the capital to Mr. White, stating that permission has been granted and the military authorities advised of our coming. Will they do? If not, what will do? Have you ever butted against a stone wall? Then, come on this tour and battle with the underlings of the Czar. The further down they are, the tougher will be your experience. I immediately wire our legation, and ask for help; and then, at the suggestion of an American here, who goes with me, hunt up a Russian, who, in Russian, writes a telegram for me to " Kuropatkine," the military governor at Askhabad, asking whether he has given permission to pass me. After paying triple for the message and answer, I am informed that the latter "will come to-night." Most un-Russian if it does! However, it does. About midnight, I am knocked out of bed, so to speak, to receive the assurance that all is well. I am no sooner asleep than I am aroused once more—this time to receive the most welcome news that all goes well at home. What blessed things cables are! So I go forward, with the assurance of good-will from all directions. B. has declined to do any of this work, trusting that he may be allowed to enter the promised land.

The steamer hence for Usin-ada leaves at ten A. M., or thereabouts. We board her about nine, fighting our way through the motley gang that always attends the advent or departure of a ship in these seas. Not one-fifth are going on her, but all push and crowd as though life depended upon their getting on board. She proves to be quite a comfortable side-wheel craft, and we are soon settled. The sea looks blue and beautiful beyond the capes, as the sun lights up the glittering surface; but around us it is covered with a scum of oil, and nearer to Blacktown it is one of the show sights to light up this floating petroleum, thereby causing the waters to blaze for miles in fierce conflagration. At night such a sight would be grand and peculiar. We are blessed, as we have been throughout this entire tour, with beautiful weather. I sincerely hope it will continue throughout the railway ride to Samarkand.

The Caspian is a stormy sea, and when you think of the countries which surround it, you are not surprised. Winds that blow over the one-time kingdom of Tamerlane and Jenghiz Kahn, over Persia and down the Caucasus, from frozen Siberia and tempestuous Daghestan, can scarce be peaceful summer zephyrs. So the Caspian is stormy, though it is smiling on us to-day. There is a volcanic island just outside the harbor of Baku, from which steam rises in clouds, and around which millions of sea birds circle. It is not explained why they select, especially in summer, such a spot, unless they have discovered the edibility of boiled eggs. What a convenient arrangement! Is it not? We have just had a good luncheon on beefsteak. It is not the first, nor will it be our last, meal on beefsteak. That, at least, is the same, or nearly the same, in all languages. Our supply of Russian is limited, and we hesitate to branch out in the bills of fare, having come to grief once or twice already for so doing. Therefore, we have rather more of beefsteak than our taste dictates. When we once leave civilization, it will be mutton, mutton, mutton.

How beautiful the water looks! The coast has sunken to that low, yellow line so familiar to you who have sailed these eastern seas. There are many sails in sight, " gliding to the distant fisheries." Yet the prospect is a lonely one— perhaps because of our knowledge of the fact that those same sails have not the freedom of the world, but must forever glide up and down, ghost-like, upon the bosom of this inland sea. A ship should, like a bird, be free ; but these are imprisoned in the Caspian. Given a love of history and geography, what can be more charming than this drifting over the world? The former peoples all countries with almost personal friends, while the latter enables one to place them properly upon the map and to fully comprehend the surrounding countries. Forever hereafter, when even casual mention is made of the Caspian, I shall see in my mind this fair, blue, inland ocean, and almost feel the presence of adjacent Persia, Turkistan, Georgia, Russia, and Siberia, while the forms and histories of those who have made them famous will come trooping over the bridges of the years in stately armies. Believe me, you can not really enjoy travel until you get beyond and away from the influence of the world's great centers of population; until you can leave the rush and unrest entirely out of your days, and allow them to glide onward, living only in the present moment. We are so far from all, and getting daily so much farther, that such things as stocks and bonds, Parliament and Congress, the repeal of the tariff, Baby Ruth and Queen

Victoria, have ceased utterly to interest us. The latter may even omit to "drive out attended by the Princess Beatrice," and we would not care. Sorry, of course, but it would soon cease to grieve us. Apropos of that same princess, I noticed not long ago some entries from her journal, as follows: "Breakfasted with Mamma; lunched with Mamma; drove out with Mamma; dined with Mamma." So it continued, day in and day out, until, toward the close of a month's record of the same monotony, came the cry: "Really, there is such a thing as having too much of Mamma,"

I have just returned from an exploring expedition, down below on this good S. S. "Alixis," which nearly created a riot. Well, when one can not read the names, how is one to know what is behind closed doors until he opens them. I opened indiscriminately, and, as I said before, nearly created a riot. A single volley of Russian is quite sufficient to knock down a stranger without using weapons. It is, indeed, a terrible language, and seems shot out of the mouth in squares, triangles, and parallelograms.

We are in the habit of classing it among those of little use, as being spoken only in an out-of-the-way country; but when, after much struggling, you have forced your way into the heart of a nation of seventy millions of people who speak that and little else, you can not but regret that it has not been considered of enough importance in the western nations to at least teach the rudiments thereof. In the greater cities, French is spoken by the upper classes; but out here, not one word of any thing save Russian; and the signs and motions that have been such an assistance in other tongues, and that we had hoped were common to all, are dead failures here. Even "pidjin" English won't work, so you may understand how hopeless and lost we feel. It is very odd, but true, that two Chinese, coming from different sections of the Celestial Empire, and speaking different dialects, can communicate perfectly by the use of pidjin English, whereas pure English and the dialects of their own language are as Greek to them.

CHAPTER VII.

" Where a silent ocean always broke on a silent shore."

Usin-ada,* June 5, 1894.

IT has taken us twenty-two hours to run the
width of this sea, one hundred and ninety-
two miles, and now we rest some two miles from
land, safely stuck in the mud.   If that is land, I
doubt my desire to leave the ship.   How hot
and how torrid it looks!   Vast stretches of low
sand dunes glow bright and yellow under a hot
sun ; a few oil tanks, some lonely-looking ships,
and a dozen or more wretched houses, with the
inevitable green domes of a Russian church
rising in their midst.   That is Usin-ada, where
we hope to enter Asia.   If all the tales are true,
we shall wish we had never attempted it.   This
is cool weather, and we are assured that it will
not be more than one hundred degrees Fahren-
heit in the train.   Next month and the month

* " Long Island."

after, the heat mounts to one hundred and forty-five and one hundred and fifty degrees. If we have even one hundred, how we shall long for a sight of these dancing, fresh-looking waters! How we shall dream, if sleep be possible, of the numerous springs and creeks under shady forest trees, in which we have bathed as children! You must come to these places to appreciate the terrible longing that the soldiers possess for the green lanes and shady nooks of old England, and the wide, pleasant valleys of beautiful France. If you were asked the locality of the desert you would immediately point to the great Sahara; but that is but a fragment of the mighty whole. To that must be added all of Arabia, all of Persia, Beloochistan, Afghanistan, and, stretching northward, the yellow waves of sand cover all of Turkistan, and stretch far into Siberia, only to change their desolation for that of the Steppes, which in their turn give place to a frozen ocean. The fertile and inhabitable portions form merely an oasis now and then, or fringe the banks of some river. All the rest, illimitable and vast, is sand—fine, yellow, drifting sand, changing every hour with the passing winds, so that the very features of a district familiar to you to-day are so utterly altered by the morrow that you know it not. Over these Russia, England, and France pour the life-blood of their best and bravest, battling ever with each other for the possession of countries over which wild nature does not intend that other than herself shall hold dominion; and their combined forces can not wrest this land from her unwilling hand. In all the nine hundred miles between here and Samarkand, there are but two or three towns of any size; the rest is desolation most profound; and yet Russia claims to have conquered it. Perhaps so, so far as the few wandering tribes are concerned; but the drifting waves of sand, the heat, and the cholera are the true monarchs of these desolate regions.

As the result of our running aground, we shall be detained and have luncheon aboard. Not a bad arrangement, as there is no good place, I am told, in that town yonder. The two hundred army recruits have already departed. The old Turk on the forward deck has gathered his harem into a dark corner, to seclude it from our prying eyes and cameras. According to the captain, these Persians are men of marvelous strength; not in the arms, but in the back. It is a common thing for one of them to carry thirty pouds—a Russian "poud" being equal to forty pounds English. Over one thousand pounds is certainly a good load. Our captain is a blonde, with blue eyes and a quick temper, and is rather indignant that we venture to doubt the statement. Abbas says it is all nonsense; that a horse could not do it. Yet Sandow lifted three hundred and twenty pounds and raised it over his head by one arm. A Turk is supposed to be able to carry a piano on his head, when once it is placed there. Take it for what it is worth. I certainly shall not try the experiment.

Freed from the mud at last, our ship steamed slowly over the shallow waters and tied up alongside the wharf. After luncheon, we started out for custom and passport inspections. The former bothered us not at all; but when we came to the latter, it was discovered that B.

could pass, permission having arrived for him, but I "must return on the steamer." The prospect outside was not such as to make me greatly regret it, but opposition to further progress had swept aside all feelings save an intense desire to enter this land if I died for it. I was told flatly to return. There were many consultations with white-capped, ceremonious officials, much bowing and scraping, much intercession by an officer we had met on the ship. I showed my numerous papers: first, my own American passport; second, my Chinese pass; third, my letter of admission from the officials at St. Petersburg; and fourth, my telegram from the governor, Kuropatkine, at Askhabad, stating that I was to be admitted. "No, it must be an error." At last, it was arranged that the chief here wire to the governor at Askhabad, and make inquiries in my behalf. So they vanished, and left B. and I looking each other blankly in the face.

"What shall you do?" he asked.

"Go back, I fancy."

"You might wait here three days?"

"Yes, and sleep on that stove in the waiting-room. It is the coolest thing in sight."

"Oh, well; you may go on. You have six hours in which to hear from Askhabad."

"Yes, I think I shall go. But out of abundance of precaution, we had better arrange matters about the things we own in common."

So we reckoned and settled up. I bestowed my new bed and cork mattress upon him as a gift, with my benediction; and just as he was about to pay me for my half in our other belongings, in came the same official, and, with the deepest salaam, informed me that it was his pleasure to allow me to pass; that the telegram had arrived this morning, but his gens-d'armes had secreted it. I bowed with the greatest ceremony, as though I believed the statement, and he retired. The whole thing was simply either a bit of blackmail or a bluff to try and scare me off, as they had done Thurston's party last week; but my insisting upon a telegram to Askhabad forced them to show their hands. How small and contemptible! How can a nation expect to be great or retain greatness that resorts to such subterfuges? I am somewhat surprised that they gave in at last. Had they kept up their usual "stone-wall" policy until night, I should certainly have returned as I came. I must, however, add, in justice to Russia, that in the Thurston matter, I have since been told that the person whom our minister instructed to apply for their permission simply "forgot to do so." (?)

There is not a place in which one can sleep here, and the town stands in imminent danger of being buried in the sand before night. I never knew such desolation anywhere as meets the eye on all sides. I wanted to stop at the old city of Merve, but am told that it has quite disappeared under the terrible sands. The heat is not unbearable if one stays out of the sun. Such winds must sweep away part of it. Our fate is settled now, and whether we cross the Pamirs or not, we shall go somewhere in the mountain and remain until autumn. It would not do to come over this railway in July, with the heat up to one hundred and thirty and one hundred and forty.

CHAPTER VIII.

7:30 P. M.

OFF at last! The officials give me a lingering glance as the train rolls away, but I am beyond their power to recall; that, if done at all, must be done by higher authorities. Trains on this Trans-Caspian Railway run three times a week only, and between here and Samarkand manage on nine hundred miles to consume sixty hours, during which time ten hours are spent in long stoppages of ten, fifteen, twenty-five, and forty minutes, sometimes at stations where no life exists and no trains are looked for, sometimes in the midst of the desert, to enable the track to be cleared of the shifting sands.

6 A. M.

Midnight was rather warm, but as the sun rose a strong wind came from the mountains of Persia; and now, at 7 A. M., it is very pleasant. I do trust that the good God will continue his blessing of fine weather—"fine weather" here

means clouds and some rain. It would seem
so far that we are especially blessed as to the
clouds, though I scarcely fancy there has been
any special order sent out in our behalf. As
Abbas expressed it, there is "no proper first
class in this country," so the railways have abol-
ished that class, and we ride second; and but for
the fact that the seats are cushioned and leather-
covered, there is not an emigrant car in our own
land that is not more luxurious. It is not my
habit to flaunt the American Eagle constantly
when away from home. In fact, to me, that
seems the acme of bad taste and provincialism.
But these notes are written for Americans, and,
if ever read at all, will be read by them; therefore I shall use "comparisons" more than usual,
in order that my own countrymen may understand more clearly this far-off land.

As I look out over the world this morning,
the desert spreads away to the westward, a dead
level of sand and sage brush; and across the
great red disk of the rising sun slowly pass a
long string of camels, led by a man on a small
donkey. Horses have disappeared. These

plains of Trans-Caspia are traversed by the camel only. Out of the other window one catches a glimpse of the mountains of Persia. B. remarks that the thermometer registers eighty-two—not bad for early morning, and yet it is very comfortable. "More anon," Sol seems to say, as he rises higher and higher over this kingdom where he reigns supreme. High noon, with the thermometer showing ninety-four; yet the strong wind which sweeps through the car not only makes us comfortable, but has carried off my white umbrella—no small loss in such a land of fire. Over all the stretches of the desert outside hangs a hot haze, through which a cross on a lonely grave looms ghost-like; majestic dust spouts travel swiftly along, while here and there a deserted village shows where man has given up the struggle. Nothing living in view, except one lonely camel! From now until four o'clock will be the hottest time of the day; but if this wind keeps up, we can easily bear it.

CHAPTER IX.

" GOEK TEPE."

" There the traveler meets aghast
Sheeted memories of the past."

"GOEK TEPE." The heart of a once war-swept country; silent and deserted now, save for our slowly crawling train and some floating vultures. Desolation reigns absolute monarch around the ruins of the fort rising yonder. Its irregular walls were deprived of half their height by Skobeleff to cover the dead—twenty thousand and more—that he slaughtered here in 1881. None were spared save the women and children and the chained Persian prisoners. Russia advanced with flying colors and triumphant music to the attack of Goek Tepe, and with flying colors and triumphant music pursued the people in their mad flight over this awful desert, hacking and hewing until twenty thousand dead told the tale of another victory for the Czar. So to this day music strikes terror to the hearts of the few who survived; and when, on the occasion of the opening of the railway, a sudden burst of melody was heard, men and women went down in the desert praying for mercy and life, so convinced were they that the sound meant death. As far as the eye can reach, rise the small clay watch-towers of the Turkomans, and the rectangular walled forts with towers at the corners; but no life or movement anywhere, save it be some moving column of dust or some wolfish-looking dogs. For nearly a week the Russian soldiers were allowed to loot this captured fortress, and three million roubles worth of plunder were carried off. These plains had been accustomed to sights of horror—Jenghiz Kahn had passed this way—but it remained for Christian Russia to eclipse all that had gone before.

Askhabad is passed at 2 P. M. The train stops there for forty minutes, for no apparent reason, unless it be an unwillingness on the part of the engine to start again over the sultry plains. Askhabad is a town of about fifteen thousand inhabitants, and is the place where five thousand of them died from cholera two years ago. There are no reports of that terrible scourge as yet, but it may come later, by which time we shall be well on into the mountains. B. has just fished the thermometer out of his bag, and reads with great gusto, "ninety-eight degrees;" but it is not uncomfortable. The sun has been hazy all day, and now has retired behind clouds of sand for good. So our dread is over for a time. To-morrow promises a scorcher.

June 6th.

A terrific wind, which invades and sobs around the train all night, as we enter the Black Desert, fills every corner of the car with sand. Still I decline to allow my window to be closed, preferring burial alive to suffocation by heat. The night, after all, has not been an uncomfortable one. Abbas arrives back from some forward part of the train, asking whether we want tea; also informing us that the kitchen is on fire. Tough work for us, if it is so. There are no eating-houses in all these nine hundred miles. We carry a dining and a kitchen car with us. You would smile at the former, though it seems fine to us here—a freight car painted white, with a bench down the center, around which are some chairs. The messes served are something terrible. We confine our orders, perforce, to beefsteak, which is well cooked. The tea and bread are good, and we drink the milk, but have long since ceased to discuss as to what kind of animal it comes from—an oil tank, I should say, from the taste. The thermometer can not rise very high if the wind keeps up. One can not see fifty yards into the desolation that surrounds him, and does not desire to. I do not believe that without shelter human life could endure for a day. There is no water in all the distance from Merve to the Oxsus. In our whole land, from the Elano Estacado to the Bad Lands, from Maine to California, we have nothing so terrible as this Black Desert. As I look from my window, about noon, it reminds me of the ocean in its wildest moments of tempest, when the spray blows high over the masts. Yet that seems all life and freshness ; this is death. A terrible sun vainly tries to banish the whirlwinds of sand that blow furiously along, making the waves with their crest of sage brush appear indistinct. Our carriage is choked with sand; and yet we have to thank it and the winds for a temperature amounting only to ninety degrees. It would have been terrible had our train been destroyed last night by the fire which attacked the kitchen.

What does Russia make by the possession of a land like this? Simply, I fancy, the holding of a watch-tower in the direction of India and the English, with, perhaps, an eye to China. There is not a bit of cultivation in all the distance traversed; no green, save in patches, on which the few miserable natives cower shudderingly. The great Trans-Asian Railway, which is to be completed in 1904, passes just north of the southern line of Siberia, and is within the Russian dominions its entire course, until it comes out on the Pacific Ocean at Vladevastock. Traveling in India is luxury itself in comparison to this. There the cars are roomy and possessed of quite decent toilet-rooms. Every

window has its stained glass to protect one from the glare of the sun. There are also the "tatties," or curtains of straw, over which water runs, and through which the hot air in passing is changed to a cool, refreshing breeze. Here nothing is done to make travel other than most uncomfortable, the cars possessing absolutely no pretense of comfort. The fruits are not yet ripe, and I can not imagine how the Russians endure the messes upon which they live, and upon which they pour quantities of liquors of all sorts, until their skins look ready to burst.

Nature remains kindly disposed in our case, as the sun keeps hidden most of the time; otherwise I do not think we could endure the heat. One poor German looked up at me this morning and congratulated me upon the weather. Then, dropping his head, he moaned out: "But I must return next month, when it will be hell, hell." So, if you must come here, select your seasons. It is too late even now; but as I have said, we are favored with a clouded sun.

"TCHARJUI."

We have just crossed the Oxsus, which here is about two miles wide. It is divided into several streams, and its waters are as muddy as those of the Missouri. At one time in its history it flowed into the Caspian near " Usin-ada," but now it flows into the Sea of Aral. What convulsions of nature must have been necessary to effect such a change! I had hoped that the influence of the great river would banish this terrible desert ; but even before our nostrils have lost the pleasant fresh smell of its mighty current, our eyes are blinded by the sand clouds, and the waves of the desert have closed in around us once more, blacker and more terrible than before, if that be possible, for now not even the sage brush breaks the dreary monotony. We are on time, however, and three hours more will land us at Bokhara. One thing is certain : it will take most serious reasons to force me to return this way. I would rather spend six months amidst the snows and in charge of the Afghans than pass over this route again. It has been without exception the worst railway

SWEEPING SAND FROM THE RAILWAY.

ride I have ever taken, and yet we have seen it under its most favorable aspects. God help those who pass by here in summer!

The winds are rising to almost a hurricane, and we are in the midst of one of those terrible sand-storms that one associates with the great Sahara. Our engine labors as though in pain, and comes ever and anon to a standstill, until we are dug out. I think six hours' halt would find a train almost buried out of sight; but we do manage to creep on now and then. Every moment or so, some louder shrieking of the elements or rattle of sand against the train causes the Russians to look up and dismally shake their heads. The sun has been hidden all day, and now all is gray and gloomy. Still, as I have said before, this is called an exceptionally good trip.

CHAPTER X.

BOKHARA, "THE NOBLE."

"Where are the kings and where the rest
Of those who once this world possessed."

June 8, 1894.

THE name of this ancient metropolis is
derived from the Sanskrit "Vihara," a
monastery, showing that even across the Kara
Kum desert the shadow of Buddha had fallen
and rested on this far northern city. Bokhara
stands in a veritable paradise compared to the
desert, and all the valley around it shows the
exuberant richness of long cultivation. Here
again are trees of some size, and the multitude
of fruit trees show what a feast the traveler
may expect next month. As one approaches
the city from the Amu-Daria (Oxus), one first
notices a stately minaret, or rather a column
more like the Kutub-Minar at Delhi than
the usual minarets of the Orient. Soon two

stately domes appear in sight, and one collects rugs and belongings in order to be ready to leave the stuffy dirty car, but the train rushes onward past minarets and domes, past houses

A "GOOD MORNING" AT BOKHARA.

and gardens, until one feels that some mistake has been made and that that was not after all Bokhara, "the Noble," yet what other place exists hereabouts? Some ten miles east of the city the station is reached. It was placed at

that distance because of the distrust of the
railway always exhibited by Orientals until they
see the cars, when childlike suspicion is over-
come by curiosity, and from the starting of the
first train until to-day, every third class carriage
has been crowded, as in India, with a motley
assemblage of natives wholly delighted with
the motion. The "invention of the devil" has
ceased to alarm, has greatly decreased the
power of the Amir, and increased that of
Russia. The Amir is prevented by dignity
from gratifying his curiosity, which is as great
as the lowest in his realm.

Bokhara maintains a semblance of independ-
ence and is allowed to do so through the policy
of Russia, whose representative, Baron Wrevfsky,
the governor-general at Tashkend, told us that
he never had and never could visit Bokhara until
Russia assumed in name the control thereof.
Were he to go now it would be most embarrass-
ing, for were the Amir to receive him as became
his state and the glory of the Czar, the people
of Bokhara would at once say, "Here is one
greater than our ruler," and would cease to

respect or obey the latter; while if the attention paid were less than that the Amir receives,
they would at once cease to fear Russia and
there would be trouble; therefore it is best to
stay away.

As long ago as the tenth century this city of
Central Asia was spoken of by travelers, and
it was old, very old even then. Here "in the
winter of B. C. 328, in the 'Royal Chase,' un-
disturbed for generations, Alexander the Great
and his officers, slew four thousand animals,
and here Alexander himself overcame a lion,
Samson-like, in single combat." Not until 700
A. D. did Bokhara emerge from the darkness,
since which time it has been conquered and
reconquered so many times that any thing like
a permanent rule was impossible. In 1400,
Timur—Tamerlane—established a Tartar dy-
nasty lasting one hundred years, after which
tribe after tribe conquered Bokhara down to
the present day, when, under Russian rule,
she is more prosperous than she has been
for centuries. But I am not going to write a

history of Bokhara. Schuyler and Cruzon have
done and well done all that.

Good Queen Bess had an embassador out
here in 1572 named Jenkenson. The eight-
eenth century held the names of but two travelers who had penetrated to this remote city.
In our century they have increased somewhat,
but still travelers are few and far between, and
their movements are known and watched. We
two are, I think, the only strangers, and I
know that I am the only American in all the
land from the Caspian to the China frontier,
from which we hear rumors of the approach
via Kashgar, hearing even their names, of two
Englishmen. Can you imagine such a state
of affairs in America, where all the peoples
of the earth pour in as free as the waters
of the ocean, though much to our discom-
fort and sometimes almost to our undoing.
Two men in the early part of this century
reached Bokhara after six years wandering
from India. Here they remained some five
months, and departed only to die in the desert
beyond. Cruzon tells of the horrible tragedy

in 1842 of Stoddart and Conolly. "Sent in 1838 and 1840 upon a mission of diplomatic negotiations to the Khanatis of Central Asia, whose sympathies Great Britain desired to enlist in consequence of her advance into Afghanistan, they were thrown by the monster Nasrullah into a foul subterranean pit infested with vermin, were subjected to abominable torture, and finally publicly beheaded in 1842." Dr. Wolff barely escaped with his life while endevoring to clear up their fates. For centuries Bokhara has been hidden as in the depths of midnight, coming distinctly into view only now and then as though in a blaze of lightning, during which has been seen the shadowy forms of Jenghiz Kahn and his savage hordes appearing on the horizon, passing with sword and flame over the ancient city, and vanishing, phantomlike, in the desert to the westward; then the city again has sunk into darkness, mysterious, romantic, and impenetrable. Our own Dr. Eugene Schuyler—he who afterward died in Egypt— visited it in 1873, under the protection of

Russia; but travelers even now are few and far between.

We were two very dusty, tired men as we descended last night from the cars at this station—descended from the comparative quiet of our compartment to the midst of such a throng as can only be found at a railway station or river bank in the Orient; a sea of black faces topped by gigantic white turbans, thousands of glittering eyes and chattering tongues, thousands of hands eager to take possession of one's luggage. No chance of hearing, no chance of progress in such cases, until you lay about you with your stick, utterly regardless of what you hit and utterly forgetful of your early religious training. You must count your packages before you leave the car, and count them every five minutes thereafter; and last night a Russian policeman came all the way to our hotel with us and counted them after we were settled. We were marked down for lunatics when we asked for baths, and were informed that here the people bathed once a week, and that we had just missed the day. They did finally find what would pass for a tub, and we were cleansed in due course of time. B. had telegraphed to an acquaintance in the town before we left " Usin-ada," but the message did not reach here until about the time we did, so there was nothing for it but to come to this house. Bokhara station is twelve versts from the city; but one must stop near the station and visit the city by carriage, as it is purely Sart, and it would be difficult to pass a night in it or get any thing to eat there.

I have to be very careful to let it be known that I am an American, and not English—that is, so far as the Russians are concerned; and I know, were it not for the strong arm of the Czar, we should not dare to enter the city. We do dare, however; and our only concern is in the choice of carriages, none of which look as though they would hold together for a ten-mile ride; and in the one we finally settle there is so strong a suspicion of bugs that we sit on the back of the seat as the safest place. So we journey onward, past orchards and meadows, down long avenues of mulberry trees, whose branches shake their berries into our laps;

through clouds of dust and hosts of natives, some riding, many taking their noonday tea and smoke at the numerous khans or cafés, where, amongst other refreshments, I see a small boy gravely carrying a pipe from one to another of the customers, each of whom as gravely takes a puff or two.

A Sart café looks like a huge, old-fashioned trundle-bed, sometimes fifteen feet square. It generally stands at the corners of the streets, and is always carpeted with fine rugs, while in one corner stands a huge smoking samovar, with its stacks of dainty teacups and pots—an Oriental never makes his tea in a metal vessel. There you may see at times crowds of men sedately drinking the dainty beverage. Whether or not tea was introduced from China or Russia, it is now the main drink of these people. I have never known them to drink any thing stronger; and I know that in the case of my guide, Rachmed, I was obliged to order him to drink cognac when he had been drenched and I feared a cold for him. These cafés are the most characteristic sight of these far eastern towns,

MARKET AT BOKHARA.

and are utterly unlike those of the more westerly Orient. But we are moving onward, past Arrab Kahns, Indian mud-houses, fields of waving grain, bowers of acacia trees, flocks of sheep, and droves of donkeys bearing stately Sarts in gorgeous colors. Dirt and dust every-where. Away to the westward, a haze near the horizon shows where lies the desert, which, thank God, is left behind for good. The walls of a mud palace, twenty-five feet high ; the minarets of a mud mosque ; the towers of a mud gateway, with mud walls stretching away on either hand, and through whose archway a long, dim vista of bazaars are to be seen—that is Bokhara, as we first see it. Through the crowds of people, strings of camels, and droves of donkeys, our carriage makes slow progress. There to our right is one of those huge tanks responsible for most of the epidemics that visit this place, chol-era preferred. Into its waters are thrown every thing, in its waters the people bathe, and these waters the people drink ; so, when this has been going on for three hundred years, its waters are ripe for most any thing. To-day they look particularly green and slimy. Crowds of curious people surround us, and near by one old man holds his particular audience spellbound as he recites in a high, shrill voice, some wonderful legend. Numerous are the vendors of fruit and vendors of sweetmeats; numerous, also, are the

A BOKHARA HEN.

turbaned Sarts, smoking or sleeping in the sunshine. As we pass down the bazaar, we are either in an intense shadow or in intense sunlight. From their little booths on either side, the solemn-faced merchants regard us earnestly; but their wares are not tempting, and there is no odor of coffee or attar of roses to induce us to tarry and purchase, as we have done through so many years and in so many bazaars throughout the Orient.   The great mosque claims our attention for a time, and as we enter the solemn silence of its cloisters, ushered thereto by a majestic Musselman, the noise of the city falls away into silence.   Sedate storks, that have been coming here from one generation to another, look gravely down upon us.   I think I have seen that old fellow, up there on that great dome, on the roof of an ancient gabled house in Strasburg. He has a look of recognition in his eye.   This mosque is old, very old.   Its spacious courts and airy arches sprang into existence long centuries ago.   Those bright blue tiles in the Holy of Holies and that glistening blue dome reflected the sunlight for the first time more than eleven hundred years ago, when England was ruled by the Saxons, France by Charlemagne; when Russia and America were solitudes most profound.

The great minaret—" Minari Katian "—which towers above the grand mosque, is still used as a place of public execution on great bazaar days, when the criminals are thrown from its summit; and I doubt if the event causes these

THE GREAT MINARET, BOKHARA.

calm Orientals to do more than glance up as the wretches come hurtling downward, or the numerous story-tellers to do more than raise their voices a little to recall the wandering attention of their audiences.   Human life is nothing in the Orient; and when one reaches China, one finds the condemned going to execution with a feeling more of curiosity than of fear, of which they seem utterly devoid.   Barbarous tortures still exist in Bokhara.   A criminal is beaten with sticks, stabbed with knives, has his eyelids cut off and eyes gouged out, is dragged at the tails of horses, and finally either tossed from this great minaret or quartered and then thrown to the dogs.

Speaking of the waters in these ancient cisterns, Anthony Jenkenson wrote three centuries ago as follows: " There is a little river running through the middle of the saide citie, but the water thereof is most unwholesome, for it breedeth sometimes in men that drinke thereof, and especially in them that be not there born, a worme of an ell long, which lieth commonly in the legge betwixt the flesh and the skinne, and is pluckt out about the ancle with great art and cunning; the surgeons being much practiced therein, and if shee breake in plucking out, the partie dieth, and every day shee commeth out about an inche, which is rolled up, and so worketh until shee be all out."

The horrible things are sometimes two and three feet long, and look like vermicelli; so Cruzon tells us. He also declares that "the most minute examination of the water under the microscope has never revealed the germ." He has a lot more to say on the subject; but it is certainly not a pleasant topic, so we will leave it.

Outside the gates are the abodes of the dead; thousands of oven-shaped mud tombs crowded one on top of the other. If the dead are so near the surface one need no more wonder that cholera—and of old the plague—is supposed to have its birth and eternal abiding place here and in Samarkand. The construction of mud walls and houses has reached perfection in Trans-Caspia. A photograph of Bokhara

would impress one with the idea that it is surrounded with a massive stone wall.   The towers,
turrets, and high walls, thirty feet in some
places, are all there, but are all composed
of mud, built up by the spadeful.   I watched
the *modus operandi* to-day with considerable
interest.   When a wall is to be built water
is conducted to the spot in ditches, earth is
carried there, and work commences.   Several
men below in the ditch stir up the mud and
water and throw it into a pile above them.
Then a man with a long-handled spade or shovel
gouges out a spadeful and passes it upward,
where another "artist," receiving it in his hands,
deposits it in its final resting-place.   So the wall
is built, shovelful by shovelful; and while the
soil is damp, it is fashioned into towers and
turrets, and sometimes ornamented into all sorts
of fanciful designs.   A wall will be six feet
thick at the base and rise thirty feet to a width
of six inches.   The intense sun of summer
hardens the work until it feels to the touch
like stone, and is almost as enduring.

All the ancient forts were built of such materials, and the Amir's palace of to-day, a very large structure, is entirely composed thereof. His highness was away on a visit, but through the kindness of Mr. L. the palace was thrown open for our inspection. It consisted of the usual number of courts, arcades, Turkish bath-rooms, and numerous small rooms, all decorated in the usual gay taste of the Sarts of to-day, who seem to me to have entirely lost the taste and talent that produced such peerless structures as the Taj Mahal, the Delhi Mosque, the Alhambra, and the beautiful Medressés of Samarkand. The same holds true of the modern architecture in India. Bokhara carpets of rare quality and great value were tossed here and there, while some absurd French glass, a brass chandelier, or some cheap English furniture, were kept carefully covered and only exposed for our admiration.

Passing finally into one of the arcades, an attendant in gorgeous robes and a magnificent turban waved us toward a table set for ten or twelve

THE AMIR OF BOKHARA.

persons, and covered with fifteen different kinds of various colored sugars, in balls and squares, cones and triangles; a plate of cherries and apricots occupied the center, and was flanked by some stale English biscuits.. We scarcely knew what to do. B. took one end of the festive board and I the other; Abbas, our guide, cooly seated himself in the center, while around about us stood some fifteen or twenty gorgeously costumed figures. Were they servants or guests? We wished to do the correct thing, but if we blundered it would be worse than a crime; so, being in doubt, we did nothing. I tried to swallow some of the "greenery, pinkery" stuff, and choked in the effort. On recovering, I found that tea had been placed in front of me, and one of the magnificents had seated himself at some little distance from the table, and commenced a confab through Abbas. So we offered him some of his own tea, and passed a pleasant half-hour, sampling every thing in sight, and are laid up to-night in consequence. It was necessary to fee some of those

men, but which one? though from the twinkling
eyes we knew all would accept it; so, laying
five roubles on the table, we adjourned to the
garden. B. begged leave to photograph our
apparent host, whom we discovered afterward
was head policeman—probably put there to see
that we did not make off with a room or two.
There was little else in sight. Consent was
given with great dignity; and during the operation I heard a scuffle in the room where we had
left the five roubles. It was too expressive to
need explanation. While the photographing
was in progress, the gardener came up and
presented me with a bunch of yellow flowers
surrounded by—of all things in the world!—a
lot of mint. I gave him a rouble, and horrified
him by immediately eating his gift. His solemn
eastern eyes could not see the long vista of mint
juleps that his gift recalled to my memory.
On our way out, numerous guards presented
arms, which we acknowledged with the utmost
gravity, having by this time become fully convinced of our own magnificence.

We had been invited by Mr. L., the political

agent, to dine with him at seven. In view of our intended departure at ten, he waived ceremony, and told us to come in our traveling clothes. He lives in a spacious mansion near the station, in one of those spreading, one-storied houses so common in this land, and aforetimes in Russia. I can not understand why the Russians so dread fresh air. When we called at his house in the morning, the outer air was fresh and delightful, but it was rigorously excluded from the house by double windows. Within it was simply stifling, and we returned in the evening with the dread of a dinner in such an atmosphere, but, on arrival, were conducted by our host to a side terrace, and there found the table. Prince G. and wife shortly joined the party, and we passed a charming two hours and had an excellent dinner. You must live on the stuff provided on the trains and at the cafés in Trans-Caspia to appreciate what that meant to us. When we finally bowed ourselves out, it was with a better feeling toward things Asian, and with us went pleasant memories of our genial host and his delightful home.   Life here would be almost imprisonment to one accustomed to the great world, yet Mr. L., a bachelor, will pass most of his where we left him.   Separated from Europe by the wilds of Russia, by two seas, by two great chains of mountains, and by that awful desert; walled in by Siberia to the north, with the Celestial Empire to the eastward, and the untrodden solitudes of the Himalayas to the south, what spot on earth can be more isolated?   True, Europe can be reached in ten days, but when the cholera comes in, that avenue is closed for months, and the cholera does come in almost every year. I think one year of life here would drive me to face a journey through the inferno, if the exit to the great "beyond" lay that way.

There is great curiosity all through Turkistan concerning our American boys who circled the the world on their wheels, and I hope, if they have not done so, that they will send a copy of their very interesting book to Baron Wrevfsky at Tashkend.

The Oxus furnishes all the water for drinking or other use for hundreds of miles around it, that precious fluid being conveyed in huge tanks placed on flat cars. Oil is the fuel most in use and is conveyed in like manner.

I am rather anxious about B. He is threatened with an ulcerated ear, dangerous at all

MUD GATEWAY AT BOKHARA.

times, though I don't tell him so, and doubly so here, where I fear we shall find no good doctors. We shall wait at Samarkand until he is better. It may end the tour, but that is a small matter. We reach Samarkand at 11 this A. M., where we shall find a doctor and where letters from home should reach us. Four hours before our arrival the mountains again loom up in the distance, not to be lost sight of for many months. On their other side lies India and in their heart the Vale of Cashmere, which D. V. we mean to see.

CHAPTER XI.

SAMARKAND.

" Look around thee now on Samarkand!—
　　Is she not queen of earth ? her pride
Above all cities ? it, her hand
　　Their destinies ? in all beside
Of glory which the world hath known
Stands she not nobly and alone ?
Falling—her veriest stepping-stone
Shall form the pedestal of a throne.
And who her sovereign ?　Timour—he
　　Whom the astonished people saw
Striding o'er empires haughtily,
　　A diadem'd outlaw !"

　　" For one touch of her hand,
I would give Bokhara, I would give Samarkand."

SAMARKAND, June 9, 1894.

I AM asked from home whether that last is mere poetic license, and whether Samarkand is not one of those places that anybody would give away.

Deeply embowered in the groves in the valley of the Zarafshan (strewer of gold), stands the poetic city of Samarkand—the home of Tamerlane, the home of all the romance and poetry in

THE GRAND MOSQUE OF SAMARKAND.

the East; where the delicious grapes and figs, peaches, pomegranates, plums, apples, almonds, and apricots grow, and dainty white mulberries tumble over the garden walls or drop on one's tea table out by the rushing brooks, always to be found in her gardens. Samarkand was old and Samarkand was beautiful before the advent of our Christ. Some say that she vies in antiquity with ancient Egypt. Be that as it may, she stands peerless to-day in this heart of Central Asia, and all through the blessing of the waters of the Zarafshan—true gold, verily, in this land of the sun. Forty-three great canals, whose combined length is over six hundred miles, flow from that river in a network over all the land, and from these a thousand branches complete a perfect system of irrigation. But around the smiling valley spreads forever the desert: to the south and west, that of the Black Sands; to the north and east, the " Famished Steppes," over which the hordes of Siberia and China have so often descended upon this Eden of the West; and if at any point the system of irrigation fails, then, like the shadow of death, the desert creeps slowly over the valley, soon suffocating and smothering all the beauty in its terrible embrace. Indeed, the very Zarafshan itself has no outlet, its diminished waters being seized and sucked under by the pitiless sands before they can reach the Oxus.* It is claimed that its waters are steadily diminishing, and, in consequence, that the oasis of Bokhara grows smaller and smaller each year, which, if it goes on, means destruction; but the traveler of to-day sees not the "handwriting on the wall."

When Schuyler visited here in 1873, Russian Samarkand scarcely existed, and was certainly not a place of beauty. To-day it is like a frame of green and gold surrounding, apparently, the brilliant oriental picture of the ancient city. From the railway station stretches away a broad boulevard, bordered by quadruple rows of waving trees; and as one enters the town, one catches sight of the governor's pleasant home on one side, with the blue and gold domes of the Russian church just beyond it, while in the distance broken arches and a wild jumble of

* The Amu-Daria, the ancient Oxus.

leaning towers tell where the ancient city is to be found.

Strangers are so few and far between in this remote eastern city, that they are subjected to almost an autopsy on arrival, in order to entirely

RUSSIAN CHURCH, SAMARKAND.

satisfy these servants of the Czar that their internal construction does not hold something that may prove prejudicial to the interests of that potentate. Strangers always arrive by the through train from " Usin-ada," and are looked for when that train comes in, which it does three times a week. We, having stopped at Bokhara,

rather than remain there another night, took a
slow train, and reached here all unexpected, to
the utter upsetting of the many officials.
" People who would come by such a train must
certainly be up to dark and mysterious deeds."
They are sure of that. Our numerous boxes
must contain gunpowder. Visiting cards possess immense importance in the eyes of these
eastern officials; and just here I present
mine. They can't read one word thereon,
but they see several names, and each one
must mean a title or denote high office. If
they make a mistake and bother some one
in position, they know they will lose their
heads. Sailing serenely on, we enter a drosky,
leaving them standing in a row, bowing deeply,
the one who holds the card being accorded the
position of honor in the center. Still they are
not sure, and all day our hotel is under surveil-
lance—we might run away with it! Passports
are delivered, and returned this morning with
the assuring message that "the gentlemen may
go where they desire, stay as long as they
please, and do what they like." Many thanks.

Rather late, though, as we are almost through the Russian dominions.   After Osh, the permission of the Czar will be worth about as much as his interdiction—just nothing at all. (You will come to the conclusion, if you finish these notes, that in that "almost through" I was somewhat premature.)

Russian Samarkand is charming, and doubly so to our eyes and bodies after the weary days just passed.   Its streets stretch away in broad avenues, bordered by four rows, on each side, of silver-leaf and Lombardy poplars.   Down both sides of every causeway running brooks go singing along.   Water, that greatest blessing to man in this parched land, abounds everywhere.   Masses of snowy catalpa blossoms shower upon us as we pass, cherries and mulberries drop over the neighboring walls, the air sweeps down from the mountains pure and delightful, and life takes a new lease.   This little hotel is a quaint arrangement of detached rooms and courts, somewhat like the Indian bungalow, yet also like the Mexican houses.   Its hostess is French, and for a time we lose sight of Russian cooking, with its attendant grease. The peace and quiet of the whole place reminds me strongly of Kandy, in Ceylon, yet it possesses the freshness of Granada. B.'s ear will keep us here a few days, and, though our time is precious, I am not sorry. As I walked to the post-office this morning, I caught sight in the distance of some domes and minarets; but that is all so far of the Samarkand of Tamerlane. We shall explore further to-morrow.

How the memories of childhood cling to one, and how strange to find the origin of one of those memories off here in Samarkand! As I rest for a moment on a bench by a running brook, away in front of me stretches a vista of sunny street. Down it comes a drove of cattle and some sheep, and behind them a picturesque boy blowing a horn. The beasts seem to understand and obey its sounds.

> "Little Boy Blue, come blow your horn :
> The sheep in the meadow, the cows in the corn."

Many a time, as a boy, I have wondered what old Mother Goose meant by that. "We

STREET IN SAMARKAND.

never blew horns for sheep and cows." I must
reach Samarkand, must leave youth behind me,
before the explanation comes. Did Mother
Goose, I wonder, find her rhymes and melodies
amongst these far eastern tribes? Did she ever
come from Boston to Samarkand? How old
every thing is! I have also discovered the
abiding place of "Balaam's ass." It is in the
adjoining lot. Balaam did not possess one ass,
but a lot of them; and they lift up their voices
in constant lamentations, coming often to my
bed-room window to pour them into my sym-
pathetic ear, a confidence that is not fully appreciated at 3 A. M. I have no recollection of any
such conduct on the part of their sedate and
dignified brethren in Egypt; but here patience
has ceased to be a virtue, and the mourning is
incessant. "Oh, my brother from that far western land, where even a little ass like me has
some chance to sleep in quiet, blame me not, I
beseech you, that I weep. You have seen how
dignified and self-contained my brethren are in
Egypt; but there we never carry more than two
of the heathens at the most, whereas here, you

see, it is always three, and sometimes four.
Therefore I weep and will not be comforted."
And so it is. One little patient donkey will
come plodding along, carrying three balloon-like
figures in gorgeous robes and towering turbans,
nothing to be seen of the beast save the tip of
the tail and the points of his ears, until one
almost fancies that the figures on his back have
consolidated their six legs into four for greater
accommodation and speed.

The way to our prophet Daniel's tomb (how
it came to be here I know not), is lined with
begging lepers. I did not know that they
were such and wondered why when we alighted
they did not crowd around us for alms. They
showed no signs of that terrible scourge, and
it was not until our return to the city that I
realized with what the hideous object approach-
ing me on a donkey was afflicted. I had seen
many at other eastern points, but none so horrible as this. It, for I do not know whether it was
a man or woman, did not look like a human being. With a river near by I should certainly put
a period to my existence, if I were so accursed.

As for Daniel's tomb, it is a long Arab-like structure, with a raised pole at one end, and is some twenty-five yards in length. He is said —here—to have been a hundred yards long when first interred, but has shrunken to twenty-five. At that rate he will be, ere many more centuries pass over him, on the minus side as to stature; still, twenty-five yards even in our progressive days can not be called undersized, and at this slow rate of shrinkage he will still be of good height long years after we have passed away into nothingness. Now, his resting-place is much affected by Sarts who desire to take tea in the country, and a samovar is steaming away just over his head.

These Sarts are a race that seems a cross between the Turk and the Parsee; with the dress and religion of the former, they possess the clear-cut features and grand eyes of the latter, and they are, I am told, much like them and the Jews, in the matter of barter and sale. The same terrible and loathsome disease, coming from the dirty water, is prevalent here as in Bokhara.

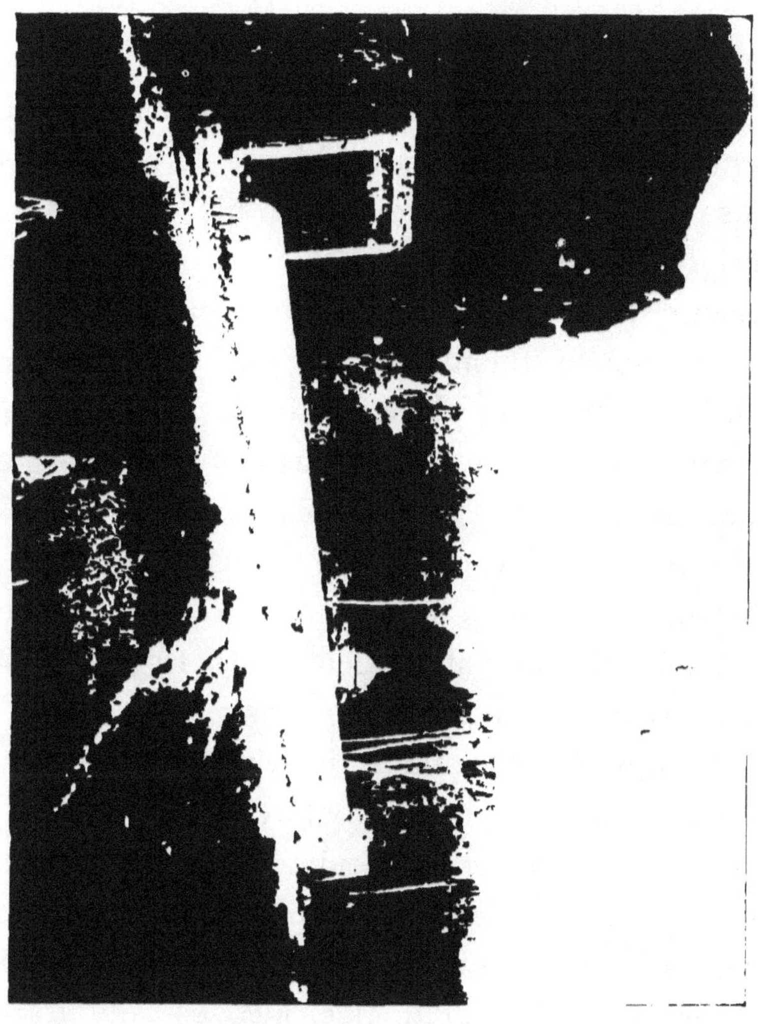

DANIEL'S TOMB.

Tamerlane sleeps, under a small black marble tomb covered with inscriptions, surrounded by his wives, his children, and his teachers. A bright blue porcelain dome that one sees rising from the midst of a clump of trees, soars above them. Water gushes around the shrine and the place is cool and fresh—in marked contrast to most eastern shrines, where the dust is generally thick enough to hide all beauty. He owes the beauty of his resting-place to the Russians, who have converted this spot in fifteen years from a dusty, arid place to a charming oasis.

In the old city there is what I have never seen in Oriental towns before—a great square, and I know of no more picturesque spot in the east. Three stately buildings, called "Medressés" or universities, rise around it, a picturesque jumble of domes, alcoves, and fretted gateways, all covered with porcelain tiling of turquoise blue and dark blue on a ground of yellow, while minarets out of the perpendicular complete the fantastic effect. The square is the great mart of the city and the crowds ebb

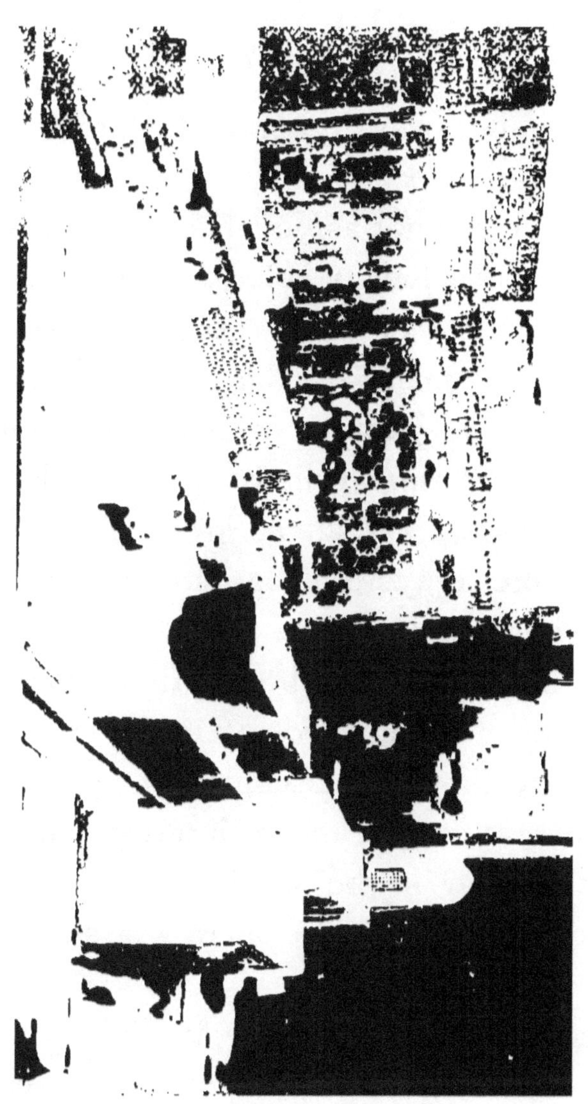

and flow and sway hither and thither like the waves of the sea.

Our west has not as yet affected these eastern peoples in their love of color, and, save in Tunis, I have never seen such gorgeousness. Here comes an old man—on the inevitable donkey— wrapped in a garment of heavy crimson, brocaded with flaring yellow figures, while from his head rises a turban of green and gold that would make a western man totter; but he sits erect. His pointed red slippers are pressed closely into the little beast that carries him forward on a steady trot. Our eyes are fairly dazzled by the kaleidoscopic changes of color. Our cameras excite much interest, but people do not appear to be afraid of them as they used to be of a pair of opera glasses in Cairo twenty years ago.

I was much disappointed at Bokhara in the display of rugs and carpets. We can see better specimens any day at home or in Europe from this same market, and I fancy that the fine products are reserved for export and the prices that are obtained thereby. We saw none of that peculiar pattern so familiar to us all as "Bokhara carpets." I am told that they are made in the outlying towns of the province. There were none even in Amir's palace.

The Russians are very polite to people they once admit to these countries. General —— sent an officer here this afternoon to act as a guide for us wherever we might desire to go, and we desire to go every-where. Backed by the power of the Czar, we broke down such doors as refused to open to our knock. This was, however, not necessary, save at an old mosque or so, where the custodian, contrary to orders, had gone off and locked up the towers. One always marvels at the continual locking up of places, by these people, that contain absolutely nothing one could carry away. A rude stone stairway is as religiously guarded as though it led to untold treasures. We particularly desired to ascend to some point from which we could secure good views of the "Medressés," of which I have spoken before. After breaking open several doors and ascending numerous dusty stairways, we reached the roof of one of them, which commanded a good view of the others, and from which we also had a glimpse of the city. Just below spread the square, humming with oriental life, and surrounded by the Medressés, with their domes,

TOMB OF TAMERLANE, SAMARKAND.

arches, and minarets, around which thousands of birds circled in the evening air. The setting sun lit up the rich blues of the buildings, and tinted even the mud city of the Sarts with a rosy glow. Away to the south rose the dome over Tamerlane's tomb, and behind the snow mountains closed the prospect. All around spread the waving trees of the Russian city. The air blew fresh and sweet, full of the odor of the catalpa. Not far to the north rose the ruins of the great mosque, the only building destroyed when Russia captured the town. It was built by the wife of Tamerlane, who never entirely finished it, and is more picturesque in its ruin than it could have been in its more perfect state. I notice that these holy houses of the Prophet, as well as those of the universities, are nearly all done in the three colors, turquoise blue and dark blue on a yellow ground. Also, that there is not the usual jumble of sacred texts thrown here, there, and every-where, but simply now and then a panel or band of them, while the other decorations are geometrical in design; the wall of Troy pattern, and many of those patterns so familiar to one on the canvas-work done at home, but all in the three colors mentioned. The domes are always turquoise blue porcelain, surmounted by a golden crescent. The ancient Sarts had better taste than most of the orientals. These effects are charming, and one can not but

SHOWING THE MOSAICS ON A MINARET.

think that, were Constantinople decorated in such a manner, it would be much more beautiful, whereas now I think that one is somewhat disappointed at the dullness of the first view of that city from the Golden Horn.

Passing through the fantastic facade of the Medressés (shown in the illustration), we entered a vast inclosed square, surrounded by small chambers, with platforms before each of them. Those were the school-rooms, and in several we found groups of teachers and scholars deep in the study of the Koran. In the center of the square stood one of those stone structures, like an open book, used of old to support some ancient copy of the Prophet's writings, most of which are now in the museums of Russia.

We have visited the celebrated "Kok Tash" (blue stone), about which some have written, but which so few, I venture to say, have ever seen. I know of one writer who plainly gives himself away by describing it as "blue." It is, on the contrary, a yellowish-gray, with nothing blue about it. In size, it must be about ten by four

MEDRESSE AT SAMARKAND.

feet, and some two feet thick, with the front covered with arabesques. It stands where it has always stood, on a platform under a pagoda, the pagoda having been for the past twenty-two years inclosed in a Russian fort, only to be entered by special permission. We had such, and were also escorted by an officer; so we not only entered, but were allowed to photograph the stone, though I fear the light was not favorable. It is said that, in the days before Tamerlane, a bright blue stone surmounted this, and on that was placed the throne chair, now in the museum of the Kremlin, at Moscow. I saw it there some years since—a square structure, heavily carved and inlaid. The Chinese lay claim to the Kok Tash, and so does Bokhara; but Russia says that it must remain here, and I am under the impression she will have her way about it. Schuyler tells us that:

"It has been common to speak of this stone as a blue or green stone, the word *kok* usually meaning one of those colours, and Lehmann (if it be not a remark of the editor) in his travels speaks of the stone as being of *lapis lazuli*, evidently from hearsay. *Kok*, however, is an indeterminate word for colour, and even means grey, as in the sport of *kok-büra*, 'grey wolf.'

THE KOK TASH.

The term might thus be applicable to marble. It is probable that the name of this stone had another origin. Baber speaks of the palace which Timur (Tamerlain) constructed in the citadel of Samarkand as being stately, and four stories high, and famous by the name of *kok-sarai*, just as the palace of Timur in Kesh was called *ak-sarai*, or 'white palace.' The *kok-sarai*, Baber says, 'is remarkable on this account: that every prince of the race of Timur who is elevated to the throne, mounts it at this place, and so one who loses his life for aspiring to the throne loses it here. Insomuch that this has passed into a common expression, that such a prince has been condemned to the *kok-sarai*, is a hint which is perfectly well understood to mean that he has been put to death.' The *kok-tash*, we are told, served as the foundations for the throne of Timur, and probably received its name from being the famous stone which was in the *kok-sarai*. The elevation of the sovereign on the *kok-tash* passed into a custom, and a legend arose that the stone had fallen from heaven, and would not allow a false Khan, or one not of genuine descent, to approach it ; and as late as 1722, in the rebellion against Abul Feiz Khan, the complaint was made that he had never fulfilled the formality of sitting on the *kok-tash*, and the rebels proclaimed in his place Rejen Kahn, who was consecrated in the usual manner."

After all, princes and peoples may pass away, but tradition remains. Tradition governs the Russia of to-day as firmly as it has governed these empires of the East for centuries on centuries; and Russia's emperor, broad-minded and liberal as he is, and possessed with a vast love for his people, is utterly powerless to change the established order of things ordained by "tradition." That name is also the last and greatest reply of the Church of Rome to all things which she can not explain—"tradition teaches it"—and she demands as blind and implicit faith in the dogmas of tradition as does the throne of Russia from its humblest peasant to its slightest word.

This day has been a fast and feast amongst the Mohammedans, every man of whom blazes with gorgeous clothing. Now and then a quiet, heavily-veiled little figure in dark blue glides along, but these figures are not many in number—the women's place is not on the street.

We spent an hour this afternoon with Count

A SAMARKAND MAIDEN.

R., the governor of Samarkand, at "Government House." Russia houses her officials well, and his quarters are delightfully situated in a park overflowing with beautiful shrubs and flowers, the former topped by our own spreading elms. In fact, the place could have been taken for American, so far as the foliage went. The house seemed mostly portico, and showed somewhat the effects of an earthquake that visited the town last winter. Those pleasant attentions from nature are not infrequent here, yet the old mosques and leaning minarets fall not.

We nave at last located Rachmed, the guide who served Bouvalot, Prince Galitzine, and the Duke d'Orleans, and shall await his coming on Sunday next. I rather fear he will prove too magnificent for his place. If so, modest Abbas will have to do, though we think it best to have two guides, if possible. We may desire to separate at Osh, where we could not find an extra one, so must perforce take him from here.

My original desire was to go *via* Kashgar, Yarkand, and Leh. I am not a sportsman, and that route offers much finer scenery, much greater objects of interest, than the barren Pamirs—a spot rich in " Ovis Poli " (mountain sheep), but dreary in the extreme; a national park, as it were, reserved by nature for her own, and also to form a barrier between the nations who surge around its base; barren of scenery, barren of verdure, barren of grandeur—desolation over all and through all; whereas the other route offers from Osh onward the grandest of scenery, though one must pass some desert. Still, the cities of Kashgar, Yarkand, and Leh, and the tremendous Killian and Karakoram Passes, eighteen thousand feet up, repay all that, and I reach Cashmere, the goal of my ambitions for years, in time to see something of it. *Via* the Pamirs, I can simply pass through that romantic vale and hurry southward, as the journey will occupy a month longer than the Kashgar route. However, this is a question I shall not have to decide until we reach Osh.

I think our sending for Rachmed has had a good effect upon Abbas. He has awakened, and spends his time devising all sorts of ingenious things, whereby our journey may be made more pleasant. Just now he brought in a tin wash-basin. He had made a cover, with a

"RACHMED."

handle, for it, by means of a piece of leather, which he had plaited down over the rim, and ran a strap through the holes in the plaits, that, when buckled, held the cover securely on. In this he has packed all my sponges, soaps, etc., and marked the leather with my name.

I expect to have trouble to-morrow with these curious bankers. I doubt if they will furnish me money, on my letter of credit, unless I wire to London, which will have to be done, as this is my last point until India be reached.

For our five hundred miles' journey to Osh, we have purchased a very good tarantass— "good" as those vehicles go. Long and low, with neither seats nor springs, it does not look very enticing; but it is all that the land affords. It is strongly built, and we trust may resist the jolting and pulling from three horses abreast that it is soon to receive. We shall sleep in it all the way, and, when our journey is over, sell the thing for twenty roubles or less. It cost eighty. I beg that you who think that a journey across our land is a bother, just to come here. If this tour through Asia does not hasten the whitening of your hair, I shall be surprised; and the bleaching will come all the sooner from the fact that all the annoyance and bother is so utterly senseless, from that caused by those in high authority to the boots which you are forced to kick as a relief to your feelings, though not from any notion that it will let light in upon his blackness of intellect.

I have just spent a most exasperating day, trying in the only bank in the place to draw money on my letter of credit. The letter is on one of the largest banks in London, and these people see that it has been honored several times in Russia, and still calls for a large balance. But no, because their name does not appear among the hundred or so printed on its extra sheet, they are firmly convinced that the drafts drawn by me would be dishonored. They will telegraph to Bokhara; and I spend twenty dollars wiring London, with small hope of reply, as there is little chance of the message getting through in a comprehensible shape. That is the best I can do. So I wait, and have waited all day. We shall probably lose three days, if I am able to go on at all. It is only within a year that this place has had any bank. A man in business here before that time was forced to be his own banker and carry all his cash in his pocket, even to the amount of twenty or thirty thousand roubles. It would almost seem that, if Russia did not make the life of her people as hard, horrible, and inconvenient as possible, she would fear the total wreck of the empire.

I may add here, that I never did get the money, and only saved delay through B.'s kindness in loaning it. I gave him a check on my home bank, which to date—October—has never turned up; but neither has B., who must be either lost in the Pamirs or somewhere in India. I wanted him to send the check to his home bank, which would put it through for collection, but he feared "it might be lost," evidently considering his own pocket, though he must almost pass through fire and flood, as a safer place than the mails of the Russians.

CHAPTER XII.

"All that tread the earth are but a handful to the tribes that slumber in its bosom."

OUT past the valley of the lepers, and running far up the side of a dusty hill, rises the famous tomb and mosque combined, called " Shah Zindeh." Early in Musselman days, Kasim Ibu Abbas came to Samarkand and preached the Koran, until here one day he was killed by some enemy—decapitated, so the story runs; but that was a small matter to so holy a man. Seizing his head, he leaped into a well, where he abides unto this day. He was expected out to assist in repulsing the Russians in 1868, but did not come ; therefore the belief that there is a greater foe than Russia, for whom he waits and watches. As we enter the portal of the mosque, grave-faced Sarts arise and salute us. Very stately are these men, and possessed, I fancy, of great wisdom. One of them advances and offers to show us the Holy of Holies. The mosque seems to consist of a long flight of steps, leading upward into dense shadows. On either side, as we mount, we notice alcoves and niches devoted to prayer, and far up we enter the shrine—which covers the well and tomb—empty, as are all such places, save for a few rugs and an immense and splendid Koran. Underneath and around are inner cells and rooms, to which the daylight and warmth never enter, and where the air is deathly with its terrible chill. It penetrates to our very marrow, and drives us forth shortly to the sunlight and life above. The old Sart is devout, but not too much so to accept our money; and leaving him, we pass outward onto the surrounding hills, graveyards, all of them. Thousands of tombs thickly covering the yellow earth as far as the eye can reach, and such lonely, dilaqidated tombs!

Some skulking dogs—or are they jackals—
skurry away as we appear, and our advent
causes a flock of vultures to rise from a newly
made grave and slowly float away in the still
air.   A more silently desolate spot I have never
seen.   .

On our return, we stop to inspect the great
mosque, built by the favorite wife of Tamerlane, Bibi Khanyan, daughter of the Emperor of China—a vast jumble of gigantic and
ruined walls and arches, so ruinous that it can
no longer be used by the faithful in prayer.
Here she was buried, and here protected by a
huge serpent, said to exist to this very day.
Certain it is, that when her tomb was violated
by those who could not conceive what use a
dead woman had with such vast stores of jewels,
this serpent waited until the robbers were ladened with the precious things, and then slew
the whole band.   There they were found next
day, and none could be induced to restore the
jewels, until one old man entered and performed
the sacred work ; but when he would have come
forth, swiftly fell the stone portal and fastened

RUINS OF THE GREAT MOSQUE.

him down forever.   The devotion of the serpent
was because of the kindness it had received from
the empress during her life; and " kindness" to-
day will reap as great a reward, though it may
take another form.   Perhaps, however, it was simply a small act of atonement toward the human
race from the descendants of that other serpent
in another eastern garden famous in history.

The legends in these eastern cities remain
unchanged and unchangeable and are told, to
the traveler of to-day as they were told to
Schuyler in '73, and to all those who came
before him to this beautiful city of Samarkand.
This seems a day of graves, but up to this
present moment they have all been such old,
old graves that they have excited no feeling
save curiosity.   Now, however, it is to be
somewhat different.   As I reach the hotel, I
meet Madam Metzler and a " friend" coming
out, and am invited by Madam to go with them
to the Russian graveyard—why not?—so I accept and am shortly following that worthy
creature through the paths of one of those
hideous "Gottes acres" only to be found

amongst those of the Romish or Greek faiths, a vast jumble of crazy iron crosses ladened with wreaths of immortelles. Madam bears a watering-pot and a rake and comes to give the sleeping "Monsieur" his weekly cleaning-up. The air of Turkistan did not agree with "Monsieur," and he soon passed to his rest, and was, so the "friend" tells me, "buried while he was *'ot.*" The friend acquired his knowledge of our tongue down near the Tower of London, where h's are considered quite superfluous—indeed, quite a matter of affectation.

While Madam rakes and waters, the "friend" takes me to the wall of the sacred inclosure, beyond which the hills fall suddenly away and then rise again in billowy waves, bearing on their crests the fantastic eastern city, and rolling onward until they break against the base of the mighty mountains. It is not, however, this panorama that I am called to inspect, but some thousands of mounds just before me and without the wall; many are well cared for, but most are sunken and fallen in, while here and there a crazy, tipsy-looking,

wooden cross makes it all only the more hideous
—"Cholera." Each and all of the thousands
there have bowed before that terrible specter
whose shadow seems to hover forever over
this fair valley of the Zarafshan.

Russia is endeavoring to destroy Samarkand's
reputation as being the birth and eternal abiding
place of the scourge. She insists that the cisterns, which are the great source of that terrible
scourge, shall be cleaned every few years, instead of once in three hundred years.

Our stay in Samarkand draws to a close, and
I can not depart without a word more for
Madam Metzler and her very comfortable hotel
of the same name. Madam is French, as I
have remarked, and has brought to this oasis
in the desert many of those charming French
ways that one remembers in the little hotel at
Blois, where the pet magpie had no tail. You
know the place. The Madam there had a
daughter; the Madam here has none, and so
we are in a measure all her children. We are
served with recollections of Paris, both in food
and otherwise, out under the bower of trees,

where cherries nod over us and white mulberries drop on our, plates. Occasionally a pet hen comes clucking around, followed by her brood of chicks; often she mounts a chair, and from thence to the table, to see that we are not more favored than herself. We are not, for she roosts in Madam's room; while, I assure you, we have a suite of apartments at the other end of the house, which spreads in a rambling sort of a way, here, there, and every-where all over the garden, inclosed by its high walls. My windows open onto the street, and as they stand wide open day and night, I am often awakened by beggars, and sometimes by a stray donkey, who thrusts his head therein. It is, perhaps, useless to say that I am awakened by the latter, if he speaks at all. Notwithstanding this Eden, I have not at all times been good-humored. Confession is good for the soul. Last night, as on many nights before, the soda water, which one must drink, was bad, and I told Madam so plainly. Madam was very "*désolé*," but that did not help the soda. Still, I have no doubt that, on many a hot day in the

farther mountains, we shall look back to Madam
and her hotel with longing and regret, as on
many days in the many months of the years
to come we shall remember it and her with
pleasure.

"MADAM WAS 'DÉSOLÉ.'"

CHAPTER XIII.

DID I say something in my notes of yesterday about Rachmed having arrived?   Did
I not bid a touching farewell to Samarkand,
to Madam mine hostess, to the native baby,
to the unnatural cats in the court-yard?   Did
I not announce that, by that hour of the next
day, we would be far away?   If so, I entirely
forgot that we were still within the Russian
possessions.   I entirely failed to understand
Madam's peculiar smile, or the fact that at
midnight she had failed to present her account;
only smiling a little more broadly and shrugging
her shoulders upon hearing that we must tarry
another day, because "there are no horses to
be had for the tarantass."   The mail moves
to-day, and there are officers en route to
Tashkend; so we must wait until to-morrow.
By paying in advance, we are comparatively
sure that we will get horses—unless—unless.

How very tired one becomes with all this delay, how impatient with this policy of constant suppression! Some time since, I wrote to a friend in London to send me two small American flags. He promptly did so, but they have never reached me, and I doubt if they ever do. None of my newspapers have come to hand, though I know that four or five each week are sent out from home. I do not think that they tamper with my letters,* although I was assured that one I sent out yesterday with a trunk key inclosed would never pass the limits of the land. "Yes" is the natural reply of the people of most nations to questions put to them, perhaps because it is a more pleasant word than "No;" but with the Russians, you are almost certain to receive the latter answer to any and all requests, though, after much argument, you may succeed in having it changed to the affirmative. This certainly comes from the fact that each rank is afraid of doing something which may offend the one just above it, and all are mortally

* I have since discovered that something like one dozen letters were "suppressed."

afraid of the all-powerful Czar. He, and he alone, has the right to think and act. All the people are mere automatons, to be worked by a wire as he directs, or, rather, as those holding high offices under him may direct. He himself is too exalted, too far removed, to ever know very much about his people.

It turned out just as I feared in regard to Abbas. Of course, we were obliged to pay a guide of Rachmed's standing much more than we did Abbas; and from the moment the contract was signed with the former for sixty-five dollars per month, Abbas, whose wages were only twenty dollars for the same period, but were all he demanded or has ever received from any one, began to get restive. We paid no attention to the numerous hints he dropped, for if a guide finds that you can be influenced in that way, farewell to your peace. The climax came on the night before we left Samarkand. It was a high festival with the Russians, and Abbas, who, "for the sake of business," has been baptized into the Christian faith, took the opportunity to celebrate it, with the result that, when he came in, after having absented himself from his post for eight hours, he was loaded with whiskey or beer; not absolutely drunk—he could have been put to bed had he been that—but quarrelsome in the extreme and very impertinent. The next morning, after the tarantass was packed and we were about to start for Tashkend, he informed us that: "We speak cross to him. Pay him little money. He no go." So we drove off without him. Of course, under the circumstances, he received no wages, and had to pay his way home. He must have greatly changed since Mr. Littledale employed him. His bills were always larger than ours, and we have since discovered that he was not exactly honest. When a servant consumes five bottles of beer in an afternoon, as he did, his usefulness is over. We were sorry on many accounts, especially as he was a handy fellow, and, more weighty still, because Rachmed speaks but little that we can understand. We were also sorry to write to the patrons of Abbas, Colonel Stewart, consul at Odessa, and Mr. Littledale, as we did; but it is best

OUR TARANTASS.

such failings should be known. Had it occurred in the mountains, we should have been in a sorry fix, expecially if he had been the only guide.

We started at last, with a merry jingle of bells and plunging of horses, and were certainly most uncomfortable until we had almost re-packed the tarantass; and I fear we saw little of the endless gardens surrounding Samarkand, so busy were we. Things were no more than settled before we reached the river, and were obliged to dump all, including ourselves, into a great two-wheeled cart, called an " arba," which is the only thing that will carry one dry-shod over the uncertain channels of the stream. And so we crossed the Zarafshan; not, however, without getting our provisions well soaked. B. nearly fainted when he saw the bread bag sailing away down stream.

The sole mode of communication between Samarkand and Tashkend,* which is the military capital here, is by tarantass, over very rough roads, where one must carry one's own food

* "City of stone."

or starve. Absolutely nothing is obtainable save tea, and now and then eggs, and those only at the post stations, which are wretchedly dirty places. The tarantass is a cumbersome, box-like carriage, with a top like a victoria, and with no springs; but is the only vehicle which

AND SO WE CROSSED THE ZARAFSHAN.

can survive these roads. In it one places all the rugs and mats he can find to brace himself with. Strong men can stand the motion, but I felt the most intense pity for one poor woman who passed us. She was going to Moscow, and had her two little children with her. The heat and glare were intense, while clouds of dust rendered all things invisible. She looked and was, no doubt, intensely wretched, and I do not see how she endured it at all. I had expected a wretched night—one must travel day and night, as there are no stopping places—but, much to my surprise, slept soundly and well. Hereafter, we shall travel as much by night as possible. The air becomes cool and the dust is much less, while the night effects on the steppes of Asia are very weird and fantastic. The plain stretches away to the northward, absolutely flat; neither mound, nor bush, nor rock breaks the dead level. The skeleton of a camel becomes a prominent object, and great numbers of turtles cross the roadway in stately procession. The moon was at its full as we passed along last night, and ever and anon long trains of camels, inward bound from Thibet and China, were sharply silhouetted upon its disk. The place was one where wolves should abound, and it would not have surprised me to have heard their mournful cry break the dead silence at any moment.

The following day, June 19th, we crossed

the Sira Daria. That river seemed weary with the weight of mud with which its waters were ladened, weary with the prospect of its long journey through the deserts. At 9 P. M. of

THE FAMISHED STEPPE.

our second day, we reached Tashkend, forty hours out, which is about as fast as the journey (three hundred versts) can be done in. We were not delayed at all. Her streets, in the Russian town, are very wide, and are bordered by many rows of trees. One can see even in the moonlight that her mansions are more pretentious than those of Samarkand, but the brooks do not go singing along as in the city of Tamerlane.

June 21st.

Hot, hot! The sun should turn his back on us now, and we trust he will not delay that ceremony. We get more than we desire of his company in Central Asia, and long often for his veiled face, so delightful in England. Tashkend is much like Samarkand—the Russian portion, I mean—but on an enlarged scale. As its elevation is not so great, it does not possess that degree of freshness so delightful in the smaller city, nor does it possess in its Sart town any such objects of interest. Extensive bazaars abound, much like all other bazaars that one sees, and become very monotonous in the long run. Nature meant all this for a desert, and a desert it was until the Russians, by their extensive irrigations, converted it into a bower; but withal you see that is a bower perforce, and would much rather return to its primitive condition. It remains as it now is under protest, and were Russia to relax her work for one year, desolation and blight would settle over all, its river being small and with no such volume of water as the Zarafshan.

I have observed that among the native cafés there is much greater cleanliness than in Egypt

TASHKEND.

or Turkey. Rich rugs cover clean floors, and the attendants seem to have washed during the present century. Still one is never tempted to eat or drink what they offer. Pass them at night, and you will see an Asiatic " Yosha-warra "—numbers of girls strewn around every-where ; and I defy the most hardened roué to go there and not feel a blush of indignation as he sees little girls of seven and eight years offered as tempting baits by their infamous masters. I also learn that sodomy is more prevalent in Turkistan than in any other portion of the world. These Sarts are not a religious people; hence one misses that most characteristic feature of oriental life—the Muezzin calling at all hours to prayer. "God is great" rarely echoes on the air here. No stately figures on gorgeous prayer rugs bow and murmur in the direction of Mecca. Not only in this, but in many other points, there is much of the charm of the Orient wanting. It strikes me, however, that the upper classes are superior to those in Turkey and Egypt. They are cleaner and finer looking, and I have met several to whom the title of gentleman could be applied. I do not remember any Turk upon whom I would be willing to bestow it.

Last night we dined with Governor-General Baron Wrevfsky, at Government House, or, rather, we dined outside the house, as the table was set in the gardens, which have been cultivated to a high state around the one-storied, spreading mansion. One of the ladies spoke excellent English, affording me a great treat, as, aside from B., I have not heard my own tongue in weeks. You must know French when you visit this portion of the Far East, and even that language is of small use. There is a good deal of it here, because of the presence of the army, but in Samarkand there were but three persons who could speak it. So Russian, in Turkistan, you must use if you do not know Sart or Persian. To my mind, there is nothing to justify the traveler in coming to Tashkend. There is absolutely nothing worth seeing.

CHAPTER XIV.

June 22d.

HAVING ordered horses for our tarantass at 10 P. M., they of course do not come, and we send after them, finally getting off at 11:30; but, as it is glorious moonlight, we do not mind the delay. Started at last, we rattle away at a lively pace, but our bells are all tied until we quit the town, from which we only proceed one station when we are stopped " until seven in the morning," by finding that two other vehicles have used all the horses. These posts are only furnished with enough animals for three tarantasses, and the waits on one's journey are sometimes most aggravating. There is nothing for it but to go to sleep, in the machine, of course, and there, in the middle of the high-road, we pass the night.

The next day is a very successful one, as tarantass rides go. We are not delayed at the posts, the horses make rapid time, and toward sunset, after an intensely hot day, we approach Kojend. Many and gorgeous are the birds, but all songless; and I have been greatly interested in the animal life of the desert; there was one strange creature—small, not more than three inches long—that crept out of the blazing rocks and stared at us. I could not make out what it was, but it looked like one of Dorés distorted shapes from Dante's " Inferno "—like the skeleton of a lost soul. Was that the road to hell, I wonder!

As we round the shoulder of a low mountain that has been in front of us all day, the entire range of the Alai spreads before us in magnificent panorama. Below, a green belt of trees denotes the presence of water—the Sira Daria; above, rise the yellow cliffs of the lower mountains; while far into the sky soars the great snowy range, which we shall soon cross. There are several peaks in sight, ranging from eighteen to twenty thousand feet. The effect is very fine. The sun goes down in a sullen glow of crimson, which gradually changes to purple, and then suddenly to night.

Twilight, there is none to speak of. We pass Kojend without stopping, save for a change of horses and tea, and a confab with an old woman and her sons from Andijan, whose invitation to visit we shall scarce accept. Then all night forward, through clouds of dust, until it is impossible to do aught save sit up and gasp. The following day brings our first real experience of post delays, and from eight to twelve we await the passage of the mails, and at four are started again, to be stopped within ten versts of Kokand, and informed that six hours will be our wait this time. It is finally cut down to three, so that at nine we rattle into Kokand, very weary, dirty men, having had nothing to eat worth mentioning for two days. Any voice that sounds a greeting is most welcome to one under such circumstances, and at Kokand we are saluted by a dapper little merchant from Moscow, who crossed the Caspian on our ship. He had passed our tarantass, and had ordered rooms reserved for us at the only hotel in the place—Hotel del Europe. These he showed us with a flourish, and we accepted with deep gratitude. They were hot and smelt of paint; were small and near the kitchen, or, rather, the porch, where the waiter washed all things in one pail, not troubling himself to change the water too often. When one has lived on liquid food for two days, principally tea, they fully appreciate a beefsteak and a bottle of beer. They also appreciate a place, be it bed or board, which, unlike the tarantass, will allow them to stretch out at full length. I slept soundly the sleep of utter weariness, notwithstanding the charms of the female orchestra, whose discords continued far into the night, finally driving the dapper little merchant to desperation and the police station for relief. Thereafter silence reigned supreme over the far eastern and very ancient city of the Khans of Kokand.

The usual Russian town of broad avenues, lined with either silver-leaf or Lombardy poplars. The usual Sart town, all a jumble of crooked streets, lined by mud houses and walls; in the heart of the whole the usual " Medressé" mosque, and bazaar; the usual picturesque crowds of dressed and undressed, most of the latter being boys. But after all, having seen Bokhara and Samarkand, you have seen all; and I should strongly protest against any one, unless they be bound for the Pamirs, subjecting themselves to that torture called a tarantass in order to see more of Turkistan.* Tashkend in no degree will pay you for the ride, and much less will Kokand, though it does possess the front and a few rooms (now used as a church) of the ancient palace of the Khan. A railroad has been projected, and will, I am told, be completed to Andijan within two years. Then the tarantass in these parts will be as a nightmare departed—something with which to scare prisoners and children into obedience.

The heat at Kokand was intense, and we decided to start for Marghilan at 4 P. M. and travel until midnight, by which time we should reach the latter town, our last stopping place before Osh. It is blazing hot as we start out, and the wind, being with us, blows heated blasts down our backs and drowns us in dust. Our pace

* I had not yet seen the grand valley of the Alai.

ANCIENT PALACE OF THE KHANS OF KOKAND.

is more rapid than heretofore. No rocks or ruts are avoided, and it is well the machine was repaired at Kokand. However, one pardons roughness here if it means progress; and it does mean progress until we roll into the last post, thirty versts from Marghilan, and are met with the news: "No horses until 2 P. M. to-morrow." We are not entirely unprepared for this, having encountered the mails, westward bound, just outside the village, and knowing that they use up the horses. There is nothing to be done save to pass the night as best we may, which I do in the tarantass, and B. on the door-step of the post-house.

Three A. M. brings in two officers, who, possessing a "podorozhnaya," take our horses, and our departure is put off four hours more. I confess I lose patience. The whole army and their relations are provided with these passes, which enable them to delay every one else. We are but fifteen miles from our destination, yet if one of us were ill we could do nothing but wait. Fact is, B. is not well, and should reach a place where he can be quiet. But no;

wait we must. I candidly confess that my experience up to date is, that the entire service of Russia's government toward strangers is "lip" service only. She will promise any thing, while she grants you nothing, nor renders you one solitary real service. There has been but one man so far in the whole land, Captain Borschefsky, at Samarkand, who has really done any thing for us. If Russia did not want us to come, she should have said so at St. Petersburg, and ended the matter there. You have seen what trouble we have had with her numerous promises, and her non-fulfillment thereof; and though we have presented personal letters from high places to the governor of Samarkand and the governor-general at Tashkend, they have done absolutely nothing to help us onward. To be sure, the latter asked us to dinner; but I feel that, with the breath of the outside world which we brought into the dead monotony of that household, we amply repaid him for his courtesy. The bows, smiles, and assurances of mutual love and esteem, and of undying remembrance, were

something wearying in length and strength;
but there it ended—lip service, all of it. When
we suggested a " podorozhnaya " to help us
onward over the five hundred miles of taran-
tassing, we were politely ignored. All our
" personal introductions," all our ignorance of
the language and strangeness to its customs,
all our shortness of time, helped us not one
iota. We two are the only strangers in the
land, yet are refused that which is granted to
every offspring or relation of every petty officer.
So we wait hours and days for horses, while
they crowd us down and back. I do not
believe this would occur under any other government in the world. As I remarked in the
beginning of this tirade, if she did not wish
us to come, she should have been decided in
the matter ; but having granted permission, and
knowing the hardships of the journey, she
should have done what she could, and it need
be but little, to help us onward. Of course,
these passes are, in one sense, like passes on
a railroad : the system could be easily overdone,
were there many travelers ; but there are not

a half a dozen in twelve months. Russia is so desirous to be well written and spoken of that a little real assistance in such a manner would gain her much. It is certainly galling for two men, whose time is limited for the Pamir tour, to be kept waiting an indefinite length of time at a wretched post station, while the nurses and children of the officers, on the strength of their passes, use up the horses between the points on the road in picnic jaunts and in calling tours between the posts. These "podorozhnayas" simply give one the right to *hire* horses ahead of the ordinary traveler; in other words, if four or five parties reach a post together, those holding such passes get their horses first. The granting of them does not entail any moneyed loss to the government.

As we approach Marghilan, soldiers come out and present arms, and before we pass down one block, a mounted policeman dashes ahead of us toward the hotel. Does it mean Siberia or an invitation to dinner? It seems he is an aide-de-camp to the governor, who has engaged rooms for us at the hotel. As we are the only guests therein, the attention, though polite, was scarcely needed.

Marghilan is a spot that could have no existence save for the irrigation. Stop that, and the hot blasts from the desert in which she is placed would burn her up in a month's time. Her streets resemble Paris in their width and magnificent lengths. Her squares, like Paris also, are superb; but when one comes to look for the houses, that resemblance ceases. If one walks around, by close inspection he may perhaps find a house or two, but he must look carefully. It is very hot here; each window is provided with a heavy felt shutter to keep out light and heat; and my thermometer rises, in the sun, to one hundred and thirty degrees, and then goes out of business. We shall press on to Osh, where it should be cooler, as that point stands at an elevation of some four thousand feet.

We certainly can not but feel pleased and very grateful for the delightful hospitality that has greeted us here at the house of Marghilan's governor. But for the fact that his house is full of visitors already, he would have carried us there bag and baggage; and as it is, we are there most of the time, and always for dinner. At our last feast—for all good meals are· feasts to travelers in this eastern land—we met the conqueror and hero of the Pamir region, Jorenoff. He spoke, unfortunately, nothing save Russian, so it was but "a glance of the eye." French, German, and also English, for a wonder, flowed around us in ceaseless chatter. One Russian countess asked me whether she would meet with such hospitality were she to come as a stranger to our land. That she would not, even were she properly introduced, I knew well; but I could not do otherwise than assure her to the contrary. However, there is much to be said in our defense. All who come here, and they do not amount to more than half a dozen a year, are not only fully vouched for, and heralded weeks in advance, but are also welcomed for the breath of the outside world which they bring with them to these lonely towns; while to our open doors come so many thousands, even from Russia, that to welcome each and all would pauperize the land in short order. Also, we have had the misfortune to be gloriously fooled by several Russian adventuresses; hence, are perhaps over cautious. Here at Marghilan comes the news of President Carnot's barbarous murder at Lyons.

The Russians have a quaint and pleasant custom of shaking hands with their host and hostess as they rise from the dinner table—a delicate acknowledgment of their hospitality. I do not, however, admire their custom of running all around the room and table during the meal, and of passing things over the board. I do not know how it may be in St. Petersburg, as my visits to that city have always been in the summer, when "society" was "not at home;" but the people we have met with are, I fancy, criterions of the nation's customs, being all titled, and mostly possessing high military rank.

We spend but two days in the town, buying tents and provisions, which we are told can not be bought at Osh. Still, we confine ourselves to the smallest amount, as transportation in the tarantass is death and destruction to all things.

Rachmed arrives with our luggage direct from

THE MISTRESS OF THE POST AT OSH.

Samarkand, and we go forward once more, leaving at night to avoid the heat, and arriving at Osh at 11 A. M. There is no hotel or place to lay one's head, save at the post-house, which we take possession of, notwithstanding the loud protestations of the dainty landlady thereof, who certainly, in addition to her two hundred pounds, possessed the shrillest voice I have heard in some time. I think, if it had not been for Colonel Grombschefsky's orders, she would have gotten the better of us, and bundled us out, bag and baggage, into the street. His orders changed her as the sun drives away clouds, and thereafter she was all smiles, and wept in my arms at my departure.

"There was music in the howling of that gale."

CHAPTER XV.

Osh, June 30th.

THIS little hamlet of Osh is placed just where the land "quivers on the rise" from plain to mountains. Jagged peaks rise around it in welcome variation from the endless steppes behind us, while the near foreground holds a rugged mass called the "Throne of Solomon." They have a habit of moving most of the personages in sacred history to this land, which must have been more remote in the days of that monarch's splendor than it is now. At all events, his throne is here. On it he gave that celebrated judgment about the infants, though now they can not show you even a piece of either child. The Greek or Roman Church would certainly be able to show most of both. The horizon is bounded on the southward by the Ali Mountains, snow-crowned and rugged, while the south-west settles down into the dreary steppes, over which we have been traveling for a week.

Did I mention the fact that horse hire is not dear in Turkistan? We paid nine kopeks a verst for three, a kopek being half a cent. I have just completed my bargain for the journey to Kashgar, four hundred versts, for nine roubles per horse. I shall need six, so that the gigantic sum of fifty-four roubles, or twenty-seven dollars, will be needed to carry me some three hundred miles, and over to that most western city of China. I have finally decided to take that route in preference to the one over the Pamirs. B. wants to spend some months in hunting, which I do not care for, and it would be stupid work for me alone in camp during his outings. So I go *via* Kashgar, Yarkand, and Leh, to Srinagar. I do not fancy the idea of a two months' journey alone, but it can not be helped.

The one or two stores which Osh possesses we about buy out. We also secure two tents and another guide. Rachmed goes with me, and one, Ham Rachoul, with B. The latter buys a very excellent fur-lined coat for twenty-four roubles. All things are cheap here, save such as come from the West. Colonel Grombschef-sky—governor of the province—is of the utmost service to us, and seems so glad to be so that we almost forget that it is all a favor on his part, and one to which we have no claim. He is the first, last, and only official in the land to render us real assistance. He asks us to dinner every day, and we do not miss any day, knowing that, when once we start southward, we shall all hope abandon as far as good food is concerned.

The governor's house stands high over the town, in the midst of pleasant gardens, abounding in fruits and flowers, and fresh with the running of many waters. Below sleeps the little town, in its bower of silver-leafed poplars. Solomon's Throne, purple in the setting sun, with its rear-guard of mountains, stands in eternal watch; while away to the westward and northward, the steppes are fast thickening with shadows. We shall start on the morrow, and therefore linger long in this hospitable mansion, leaving it and its master with many thanks and regrets, taking with us many memories of its coolness and rest. and of his warm, generous heart.

OUR PACK.

July 1st.

It is 10 A. M. before our "pack" is in starting order and we get under way for the wilderness. I have six horses in my train, and B. nine in his; but I shall only keep this lot until Kashgar be reached, a fortnight hence, while B. must keep his until his journey to Gilghit* is an accomplished fact. We have packed every thing possible in boxes or thick bags, and so have little trouble in arranging, and these Sarts rope them to the pack-saddles so securely that they arrive at our first point, Langar (twenty-eight versts), in good condition. I have had cases in our Rocky Mountains ruined the first day by carelessness in packing. Langar is nothing save a "Membashics" tomb and a stream of running water. The first, though it is picturesque, with its broken dome and black plume, we might do without, but not the water. Only those who have been off in the desert appreciate what a blessing water is to man and the world. It means life. Here, at all events, it does, and to-night it takes the shape of a sparkling brook. There is some quarreling over the preparation of the first din-ner, but we get it at last. Soup, canned salmon, tea, and rice make us happy and sleepy, and I do not mind the fact that my camp bed has

* The northern outpost of Great Britain in Cashmere.

an iron rod that before day nearly breaks my back. How deliciously cool the air blows through the tent! which, by the way, is not our own—they are of canvas, while this is one of those great "yourts" of the Kirghiz, a circular structure of some ten feet in diameter and as many high. It is not long before silence settles over our first night in camp in Central Asia.

Half-past four brings daylight. Chattering Sarts, Rachmed and Ham Rachoul making the fire, neighing horses, etc., make sleep impossible; and we order in the tea and boiled eggs. Both are delicious, and of the latter we consume six apiece. It is never well to start ahead of your camp, if you desire its arrival before midnight; but once get it under way, and it will move steadily forward all day. So we wait and start with it, the result being that we reach Gulcha about the same time. En route, two passes are crossed, one being higher than Mount Washington. The views are beautiful, and ever and anon we catch a glimpse of the vast fields of snow, still three days away. The forty versts to Gulcha are covered in about nine hours, and as we descend into its valley we are met by a messenger from the Membashie.* Colonel Grombschefsky had warned him of our coming, and we find him awaiting us on the further side of the rushing Gulcha River. After a dignified oriental salute, he conducts us to a yourt like the one of last night, whereupon I am ashamed to confess that I stretch myself out and go sound asleep in the presence of his highness. But one meets so many highnesses, and I am so weary, that nature takes matters into her own hands.

I have sent Rachmed into town with my bed to have those rods cut out. It is an ordinary camp bed, iron and folding. It will, of course, weaken it, but I can not sleep on it as it is. Now I shall have canvas tied over the whole. We were strongly advised not to sleep on the ground, or we would not have bothered about beds.

My first papers from home of May 20th reached me at Osh on the 30th of June. I shall have no more mails until Kashgar be reached. It is rarely in the world of to-day that one finds a journey that, so far as mails

* A chief amongst the Kirghiz.

are concerned, burns their bridges behind them for two months.

Let me recommend to my men friends to bring a bath-robe or so when they follow in my footsteps. (Let me recommend to my lady friends to stay at home.) I really think it is more useful than any thing else I possess. For instance, to-day, when I wanted a dip in the Gulcha River, half a mile off, it came in most handily, and the natives evidently considered it a robe of state. Between that, my yellow umbrella, and my spurs, I can see that I stand high in their admiration. However, it is the absolute comfort of a robe that I mention now.

We have set Rachmed and Ham Rachoul to making chicken soup. I fancy it will be ready to-morrow. Concerning camp life here, I think that one coming to these countries should in our own land lay in a supply of canned goods. They can not be gotten in Russia, and most of Europe seems prejudiced against them. What would I not give for some canned fruits—peaches, pears, apricots, etc.? Not jams, but some marmalade. We have been able to procure a little canned salmon and venison, which seems so ancient that we are almost afraid to eat it, and I think with envy of all in our stores at home. So far, except at some post stations, we have always been able to procure eggs and milk, which, with tea, will keep a man going, though the desire for meat will be unpleasantly strong at times; but one must become accustomed to go without that. I fancy, as I go forward, I shall have but little thereof, save in the cities, and I fear Rachmed could not cook it if I had it.

I can not but compare the industry and promptness of these guides and packers with those in our western mountains. These move quickly and do our bidding as ordered. There is no delay in packing and starting; while with our western "gentlemen," who are at all times better than their employers, things are far different. I shall not forget my last visit to our wilderness. The head guide, "Handsome Jack," posed most charmingly against the rising moon, while "Pretty Dick" moved quickly only when there were girls in sight, of which there seemed always any number when he was known to be coming. If we ordered an early start, they raised their eyebrows in polite surprise, and we, if luck went well, got off at 9 A. M. Here a five o'clock order for moving is generally obeyed to within half an hour, and these men are not above their business. As I sit in my yourt writing this morning, their clatter and noise is tremendous; but I notice that the work moves steadily forward, and now Rachmed appears at the door, and, with a deep salaam, announces that all is ready, and we move onward more and more into the heart of the mountains.

This is our last yourt, and to-night we shall raise our own tents and be our own landlords. I find that the life is agreeing with me wonderfully. I sleep like a top and can eat almost any thing, all of which, I have no doubt, will be entirely upset by a return to the delights of civilization.

The erection of a yourt is no small undertaking. We had expected to see no more of them, but the one of last night reached here almost as soon as we did. It required a horse and a cow to carry it. The rack-like framework is first erected in circular form, after which a

THE FRAME OF A "YOURT."

dome-like top of staves, open in the center, is bound on with rope. Around the frame is stretched a bamboo screen, and over that skins

are drawn and bound down. A door gives
entrance to the structure, which no storm seems
able to blow over. They are cool in summer
and warm in winter, and the opening in the
top allows one to build a fire in the tent in
cold weather. I trust I may never be called
upon to inhabit a place less comfortable, in
which case I have no dread of my future
habitations.

These regions are alive with our domestic
pigeons. B. has killed two just now, which
will come in well for dinner, but it seemed
cruel to kill them. I felt more resentment than
pity when I discovered that they were too tough
to eat. I notice some birds of most exquisite
plumage. One on a rock near by is clothed
as though condemned to the penitentiary for
life, and it is in fact called the "jail bird."
The black and white stripes are of equal
breadth, and pass around the body and wings,
while the neck, head, and comb are of a brilliant brown. Another is of a turquoise blue
and gold; while a third has wings of a moss
green color, which shade off into the olive

of its neck and deep crimson of the head and breast.

All the cows here are mares; at least one would so judge, as we can get nothing save koumiss, a liquid which, like the Mexican pulque, I can not drink.

Our route to-day covered only twenty versts, which left us most of the afternoon in camp. One must—on account of the horses—regulate his journeys by the grass to be found, of which there is not much in these mountains. The air does not turn fresh at sunset, as in our Rockies, but is cool and balmy, and becomes cold before daybreak, when a strong wind generally precedes the rising of the sun by an hour or so. Last night I slept under two blankets.

This is the early morning of July 4th, and though I am some hours in advance of home time, still I doubt not but that the inevitable small boy across the water has already expressed his approval of the act done in the last century.

CHAPTER XVI.

July 4, 1894.

"BETTER twenty years of Europe than a cycle of Cathay." Perhaps so, but Cathay in these solitudes as the sun rises is certainly very beautiful, and I doubt not that the human body would stand the cycle here better than the twenty years in the gay cities of the world. Man seems to come in close communion with the great hereafter in these mountains, to attain, as it were, even here on earth "a closer walk with God." All the littlenesses and small-nesses that may have beset his life drop away and are forgotten, and I think if he were called to the Divine Presence from the heart of these hills that the recording angel would wipe out much of his indebtedness, because of his for-giveness of all below.

One soon adopts caravan hours—asleep be-fore nine o'clock, awakened before 4:30 A. M., which does not seem so very early, and the air at that hour is too full of life for sleep—"death's younger brother"—to be indulged in. Here come the horses back from the higher mountains, whither they went at sunset in search of grass. By 5:30 we are again en route.

Rachmed has been giving us his experience in Paris. Between his half a dozen French words, his flow of Sart, Persian, and Chinese, intermixed with many gestures, it was intensely funny. It seems he was most attractive to the women, who gathered around him in such flocks at the restaurant that he could not eat his dinner, and, therefore, a la Turk, knocked down one or two of them, and was promptly jailed by the police. It took several linguists from the university, together with Bonvalot, to release him, after which he declared, " Paris finish beaucoup femme, beaucoup femme," and left for London, where he was unmolested. He is not the first, as he will not be the last, for whom the women of Paris have proved too much.

There was a great commotion just now when

it was discovered that " Balaam's Ass " (our one donkey) had devoured the chief's dinner. That donkey is wise beyond his generation. I notice that he eats every thing in sight and rests on all occasions.

So far, this road could be traversed by the tarantass. In fact, the great two-wheeled cart, the "arba," does come, and an army could easily be marched swiftly southward. It is rather a marvel to me that Russia has not built a railroad at least to Gulcha.

Thirty-two versts is not very much, but one must search for pasture, and, when found, there abide, be the journey long or short, for the horses' sake. All these thirty-two versts are over a jumble of mountains and valleys, for which even nature appears to have little use. No life, animal or vegetable, is to be seen anywhere. Even the wandering Kirghiz appear to have given up in despair. About noon, we pass "Surfe Kuhrghan," a desolate, deserted, and useless fort, useless even to Russia. Around its base rushes the Gulcha River, while the red cliffs rise behind it, to be backed in

turn by the higher mountains, over which the
Terek Pass is laid out; but because of the
mud thereon, we must go over to the Taldek,
and thereby add a day or more to our journey.

Our camp to-night is by the Taldek River,
and in a basin of red rocks.   B.'s hunting
guides meet him here, and our separation is
near at hand.   The prospect of parting seems
to have affected Ham Rachoul more than any
of us; or is it the recollection that, for all the
months that he will be absent, he has left his
wife but two roubles for her support?   At any
rate, he sits out there on the mountain side,
deep in reverie of some sort.

AKBOSAGA, July 7, 1894.

A high valley, its altitude somewhere between eight and nine thousand feet. In appearance it greatly reminds me of the Engadine.
To-day we cross the Taldek Pass, but it is
only four thousand feet above us.   The Alai
Valley lies just beyond.   In the Sart language
the word means " Paradise," but any place in

HAM RACHOUL IN REVERIE.

this land that possesses water and grass is a paradise.

Crossed the Taldek Pass, eleven thousand, eight hundred feet in altitude. Some fine scenery. The passage is very easy at this season. As we descended the south side, the entire range of Trans-Alai Mountains spread before us—a very magnificent sight, not surpassed, as a whole, on the globe.

B. turns southward here, and I go eastward. I confess the prospect of the next month and a half alone is not a cheerful one. It will be broken, however, at Kashgar, Yarkand, and Leh, where I shall find the English tongue. I am camping to-night in the midst of the first large Kirghiz town that I have seen, and a strange sight it is: numbers of yourts, surrounded by groups of fantastically dressed women and dark-looking men; herds of horses, cows, and camels wandering hither and thither over the rich grass. The Kizil-Su (Red River) flows, copper-colored, before my tent, while over its valley rise the mountains in snowy masses until lost in cloudland. It is only the strong arm of Russia that protects me here. Two months since, a Russian traveler, with his attendants, was murdered on the Terek Pass by their guide, one of these same Kirghiz; but Russian vengeance found the murderer in short order, and he now awaits the rope at Marghilan. They seem friendly here now, and have just sent a deputation to me with some fresh milk, which is most acceptable. Rachmed takes great delight in trying to induce me to drink koumiss and other stuffs, but does not succeed. So the milk is most welcome. When the Kirghiz presented it, he placed his hand on his belt and made a bow that with us would convince one that he was troubled with violent disorder in that portion of his anatomy, but here it is a salutation denoting the deepest respect. Rachmed informs me that he, himself, not the Kirghiz, has two wives. The first lost a leg soon after marriage, and was "not much use," so he married another. "With three legs, the two get along very well."

I met the post going west to-day, and sent home a letter. No matter how remote, one always meets with some touch of the outer world near him.

It is not altogether a pleasant thing, when you are up and ready for a long ride, to find that the horses are off in the mountains, and to be told that the Sart in charge has probably gone to sleep and won't wake up for hours. Such is my case at present. There is absolutely nothing to be done or said about it, and it is certainly no use to get angry. Heaven knows when my handful of horses will become separated again from the thousands of animals gone from here to the mountains. Of the multitude on the plain last night, nothing now remains save some old men and women and (I should not forget him) the chief of the tribe, who, in gorgeous raiment, came to call this morning. The matter of the horses is more serious than I thought for. It seems that the man in charge slept on here in camp, while our animals wandered off with the Kirghiz horses to the hills. I suppose they will return to-night, and at best it is but a day lost; but they may wander backward toward Osh.

They are finally found, and we start some three hours late. The Sart who is to blame is in mortal terror lest I write to Colonel Grombschefsky, which would mean fine and imprisonment for him. I shall hold it over him to insure no repetition. The loss of one's horses here is much like being dropped overboard at sea.

My route lies directly eastward through the Alai Valley, and I shall stop to-night at the Russian frontier fort of Irkeshtan. This is my first day alone. All the morning I have jogged along in silence, Rachmed in front and the pack behind, none of them speaking enough French to render conversation possible. It is not cheerful work, but it can not be helped; so I spend my time between admiration of the mountains and the flora. The latter is very extensive. The "edel-weiss," so sought after in Switzerland, grows all over this valley; so does the "gentian" and "forget-me-not." There is no wood anywhere, and Rachmed, in the absence of the pack, is forced to make tea over a fire of manure—not a very rapid operation. How quiet it all is! Only he and I alone here in all this wilderness! The grass is deep and green and the brook gurgles onward singing. Around the shoulder of a great rock a solitary camel makes his appearance, to be followed in sedate fashion by another and another, until I am surrounded by a vast caravan, when that which was lonely and deserted becomes all alive and bustling, with the life of one of those moving cities.

NOORAII, Sunday, July 8th.

The entire ride yesterday was over a succession of passes and mountains, enlivened here and there by a deep green meadow with a pool of clear water in its midst. Invariably in every such oasis we met with one of those gigantic caravans which for ages have trodden these paths from the Celestial Kingdom to the barbarous west. One of them to-day must have been composed of some five hundred of those patient "ships of the desert." The scene was most picturesque and patriarchal. Near the pool were the huge bales of goods, watched over by turbaned and bearded figures,

while the tent of the " Membashie " rose a
blue patch from the water's edge. Around
soared the gigantic mountains, green merging
into grey, grey melting into the everlasting
snows, which showed sharp and clear against
the intense blue of the sky.   Hither and thither
in couples or strings of fifty or a hundred, noise-
lessly moved the camels, each division led by a
stately patriarchal figure, which, if it caught
your eye, immediately bent low in deep salaam.
Rachmed says that the camel suffers much
from rheumatism, hence this exercising after a
day's journey.   Certainly one would fancy that
if any disease troubled these beasts it would
be that.

Later in the day we crossed the two branches
of the Kizil-Su River, the waters of which, always as red as copper, and full of sand, are often
in beautiful contrast with the blues and greens
of the mountain brooks.   It was rather difficult
work at times getting the pack over.   All of
them hesitated save Balaam's Ass, who always
made straight for the flood, and never seemed to
wet any thing he carried.   However, his burden

has been so greatly reduced that he might almost be considered a "parlor boarder." He certainly boards near my tent, and enters into confidences two or three times each night, so that I fear that I offer up a prayer that he may not find his voice—one must sleep you know.

There are on the maps two "Kizil-Su" Rivers, one flowing west from the Alai and joining the Oxus, the other east and entering the Kashgar; so that the waters of the first, such as escape destruction in the black sand of the desert, enter the Sea of Aral, while the other flows onward to the Pacific Ocean.* The gorges of the latter are very grand; great masses of red sandstone, carved into fantastic shapes by the passing of winds and waters and the flight of time.

To-day we enter China. Rachmed regards her people as of those not to be trusted, and at his suggestion I have armed myself with two revolvers instead of one, with, I fancy, greater danger to myself than to any one else. At present I am left high and dry on a stony island in the

---

* The outlet of this "Kizil-Su" does not seem to have been fully determined, though it is believed to flow into the great "Yellow River" of China.

middle of the Kizil-Su River, with nothing in the shape of baggage save my kodak and a yellow umbrella. The pack has gone forward to effect a passage, and I will be "sent for." If

"IRKESHTAN," RUSSIA'S LAST FORT.

not, I shall return to Fort Irkeshtan, which we have left but two versts behind, and in doing so bade farewell to all that is Russian. Whatever I may think of Russian methods of government, I have nothing save praise for Russian hospitality, from Prince Galitzine* at St. Petersburg to the little yellow-headed custodian of this extreme outpost of the great empire, as he stood, cap in hand, bowing an adieu. He treated us to our last samovar and cakes, and bestowed upon me two chickens and a half a dozen eggs, a present for which he absolutely refused all payment, and which, let me tell you, in this barren land, was more appreciated than the most dainty dinner when in Paris.

The river is crossed at last, and I turn to take a last look at its red tide, its crimson rocks, its snow-clad mountains, and then move onward into China. Up the valley of a dried-up creek moves the pack, and Rachmed and I follow. Yesterday all was life and movement, green grass and rushing streams, while the air was ladened with the perfume of many flowers. This valley up which we are traveling is barren of life of any sort, save that shown by some straggling sage bushes, while here and there the skeleton of some dead camel grins ghastly from the yellow sands. The scenery loses its

---

*The head of that noble house, *not* the degenerate scion lately "sold out" in New York because he could not "live up to his blue china."

interest, and, dropping my bridle, I allow my horse to plod onward (which he does with his eyes shut, apparently, as he shortly runs into a rock), while my thoughts quickly span the distance between here and home; but one does not dream long in such a place. Down the gully comes a hot wind that would be suffocating but for a counter breeze of delicious coolness from the Alai Mountains behind us. Onward for three hours we plod, until finally a wide green valley opens out, and the horses press on, hoping for water, only to be disappointed— nothing in it save sand and sage brush. It is not until another hour is passed that we reach the Chinese post, Ulkchat, where we remain for the night. It is the extreme western post of the Celestial Empire, and evidently considered amply able to protect itself, as not a soldier is to be seen—nothing save a lonely camel near the fort, who growls at us as we pass, fearing to be disturbed; but with a clean tent to sleep in, he need not fear that I want that dirty hole, and Rachmed and the Sarts always prefer to sleep in the open air.

Ulkchat is situated in a green oasis, with

many rushing brooks around it, and might be made a delightful spot; but the world has enough and to spare of such without penetrating the silence of these mountains.

There is such a thing as having too much

THE FIRST POINT IN CHINA.

of patriarchal life, as I discovered on awakening from a nap this afternoon and finding a bearded goat in my tent, calmly devouring a trunk strap. He moved off with extreme dignity when I, shameful to relate, kicked him out.

Rachmed has been in for his usual evening

chatter, and though his words are a grand mixture of a dozen languages, he manages to make himself understood. My not being well to-day furnishes him with his text. He says Prince G. was sick all the time, and the Duke D. ditto. His confab is interrupted by the arrival of the " Membashie," or village chief, who brings a sheep to me as a present, and in return for which I give him a silver watch, which makes him strut like a turkey cock. He does not know how cheaply they are made in the West, nor that I have laid in a supply for just such occasions. It is not much fun being ill, but I am alone to blame. I knew those greasy cakes at Fort Irkeshtan would not agree with me, but nothing but tea and canned things for days made me forgetful.

In my notes of yesterday, I find I was entirely wrong. This is not the Chinese fort Ulkchat, but a stopping point called the " Fort," a mere Dak Bungalow, so called even here, which is our first evidence of Anglo-Indian influence, even though we be so far off that frontier.

July 9th.

We lunch to-day in a grove of old trees, that, though poplar, have much the appearance of the olive, and I think the garden of Gethsemane must have been much such a spot, not only in the days of the Passion, but

centuries after; and, indeed, that sacred bit of ground would look to-day much as this does, had it not been desecrated by the wall which incloses it, and by the many gaudy Roman shrines. To my mind were it open and free to all, were its fountains the trysting place of all nations, and its trees still shelters for the camel; if one could in fact wander under their venerable shade alone and with free rein to such thoughts as must come to the hardest of heart there, I think Gethsemane would be a much more sacred spot than now, when one has sometimes to fire rocks over the wall to awaken the sleeping monk, who, when he unlocks the low door to you, nearly knocks you over by the smell of garlic and of his foul person. Here in the heart of Asia this solemn spot is clothed in silence, save for the murmur of the river, and the grumble of some camel from a caravan that I can just discern through the trees, whose knarled and knotted trunks and dense foliage have afforded such a delightful hour of repose after a morning's journey through the heat and sand, and before an afternoon's ride of the same kind. I shall always think of it as my garden of Gethsemane, only here there has been neither agony, nor sorrow, nor the memory thereof— simply dreamful ease.

We reached our last crossing of the Kizil-Su at about 2 P. M., and as Rachmed had no notion as to the ford, a Kirghiz came up on his camel and volunteered to pilot us across, which he did successfully. As usually Balaam's Ass insisted upon staying in the water and had to be sent back after. One can not blame the beast on such a hot day. I would like to do the same myself.

Stopping for milk at the Kirghiz village, I was invited by my guide to enter his yourt (also called " Kibitka "), an invitation I accepted, though with some trepidation on account of the dirt. He had to kick aside several mangy dogs, and push away the baby camel, which, from the inside, blocked the entrance. How filthy every thing was! yet one of the women drew out for my seat a rug that would honor any drawing room at home, and then offered me a draught of clear, cool water in a dainty porcelain cup. Goats walked in and "bahed" at me ; a dirty cat was rather more friendly than I desired. The people sat in a circle and were politely curious. I say "politely," because they could have given lessons to many at home, who, perhaps, think they do not need such instruction. The women wear towering white head dresses, which are generally clean, but the remainder of each costume is generally composed of one dirty garment. The men "at home" wear as little as possible, but when out, wear, even in this torrid weather, a sort of thick double gown and a heavy felt hat. On leaving, I induced them to allow me to kodak the entire establishment, a picture which I hope will develop well. They are certainly a very different race from any I ever saw before. Rachmed tells me that they live here in a sort of imprisonment. The Russians will not permit them to enter their paradise, the Alai, and the Chinese keep them here. What a life! The place is on the banks of the dirty Kizil-Su and surrounded by towering yellow cliffs that blaze like a furnace from early morning to nightfall, and then the winds sweep down in icy blasts from the snows above, making, by their extreme contrast to the day's heat, a place of torture.

We ride onward for two hours, over yellow, dusty rocks, and in a heat more oppressive than any I have yet endured. I neglected to mention our passing the Chinese fort Ulkchat,

MY KIRGHIZ HOSTS.

but the description I gave yesterday before
we reached it will answer—"a wretched, dirty
mud square," with no sign of life save the flag.
If soldiers there were, they must have been
sound asleep.   Not even a barking dog greeted
us.

CHAPTER XVII.

AND now I have to record a disappointment and a failure. I have dreaded it for
several days, but had hoped to ward it off. The
heritage of a fever which almost laid me low
some three years since is an abnormally sen-
sitive digestive apparatus. The doctors call its
exhibitions "intestinal dyspepsia." It had not
visited me for months, and I had believed it was
a thing of the past. I must have taken cold at
Akbosaga ten days ago, as I noticed when I bade
B. farewell that I was not in prime condition, but,
not wishing to spoil his trip, said nothing, and
came on alone. That night I grew worse, but
struggled onward until yesterday morning, when
Rachmed asked me if I were not ill. I had
scarce sense enough left to tell him to take
the backward route for Osh. I had discovered
that morning that my stomach refused even my
old standby, "milk," which left me nothing save

pure brandy with which to go onward upon, and
that, I had been assured, could not be obtained
in Kashgar, and my supply was almost gone.
What a situation!   Alone in a Chinese desert,
whose blazing cliffs almost grilled me with their
reflected heat; not a mortal with whom I could
speak save Rachmed, and to him only a few
French words, eked out by gestures which he
never understood; before me a two months' tour
ere I could hope for succor; behind me a ride of
eight days to Osh, where I should be sure of
finding rest, aid, and sympathy!   But even then
I hesitated.   I had so longed to make this tour,
so longed to see the Vale of Cashmere; and
to abandon it now, when all was plain sailing!
It was almost more than I could bear to think
of; and all that morning, as I struggled through
that blazing desert, I battled against surrender.
But it had to come; and it seemed as though
another will, another voice than my own, ordered the return.   So we turned, and after some
hours reached the Kirghiz camp where we had
been entertained the day before, and where I
went to bed for thirty-six hours.

Now we are moving backward toward the high, cold valley of the Alai. Of course it is best. Onward certainly meant death to me, and I have other work to do before I can consent to that. I can never speak of Rachmed's kindness and sympathy, when things were at their worst, without deep feeling. To-

RACHMED.

day should have been one of great heat, and therefore of intense distress for me, but during the night a high wind arose and is still blowing. It has lifted, carried far above us, and filled the sky with a gray veil of sand, which has shaded the sun and made the day bearable. To-night we shall put up in the grassy dominions of the Membashie to whom I gave the watch. We met him just now, and he pulled it out on me, explaining that it would not go!—all nonsense; however, I gave him mine in exchange, and am now wearing his, which does go. He simply neglected to shake it. Early day brought the same individual squatting before my tent and gravely regarding his watch. It had stopped again, because he had not wound it. The old man either considers it supernatural or as possessing perpetual motion. He came in state on this visit, attended by two or three of his cabinet, one of whom, at a wave from his hand, presented me with three eggs, and another with a bowl of milk. You can not imagine, unless you have been situated as I was, how very acceptable those articles were. I was strong enough, in consequence of being able to avoid the eternal mutton soup, to take a long day's journey. I can see that I have risen greatly in the estimation of Rachmed and the Sarts of my camp by the presentation of that watch. Rachmed says that Prince G. never gave such "valuable presents." The watch cost about $3.50; hence I wonder what sort of presents Prince G.'s could have been.

July 11th.

Russia viewed from the high plane of European and American civilization, and Russia viewed from the high plains of China, present two very different pictures to the traveler. When I reached her outpost, Irkeshtan, this morning, after a hot journey over the desert, it seemed the acme of all civilization—a very heart's content; and when I passed among the chickens and crows in its dirty courtyard and on into its low, dark, and dingy rooms, there, seemed a place I should like to linger in; and the slovenly, ragged little keeper a prince of entertainers. I do not think that tea ever tastes so well as when the water comes from a samovar, and that particular, much battered, and damaged samovar gave out most delicious hot water. The room was dark, and oh, so cool after the blazing sunlight. Again the Emperor's picture smiled benignly down upon me, and I felt that at least there was a power that could be applied to in case of necessity, and with some chance of succor being granted; Russia, even in that remote outpost, seeming very active and stirring after the death-like silence of Western China, whose last fort, Ulkchat, I left this morning, rising a yellow mud structure, over which silence and decay held perpetual sway. Fort Irkeshtan was, on the contrary, a commodious white building, which gave evidence of occupation. There were thirty-six Cossacks there, though, aside from mine host in the post-house below the fort, I did not see one. I was not permitted to enter the military structure; only the post-house, whose custodian informed me that he was not married, and assured me that there was not a woman on the place. (It is marvelous what a conversation can be carried on by gestures.) I am sorry to say that, as I departed, I saw two Kirghiz women peering from behind the door of a yourt. It is not the first instance in which curiosity on the part of that sex has utterly destroyed the reputation of our race.

The journey backward into the beautiful Alai

Valley is picturesque and interesting. We forded the Kizil-Su no less than six times, getting very wet once or twice—no pleasure that, in its nasty red waters. The cliffs become very wild and rugged as we mount, until finally we reach the upper table-land of this valley of paradise. Once more the snowy mountains stretch away before us; once more the hills and valleys are covered with the patriarchal tribes and with flocks and herds. We have come for hours over beds of flowers, and to-night, as I wait for my dinner, my horses are taking theirs off of masses of mignonette, while the little donkey rolls in a bed of forget-me-nots.

July 12th.

We have been delayed some time this morning, and all because Balaam's Ass discovered a sweetheart somewhere near, and went off by night to visit her. How to discover our wandering Don Juan was a problem, and I was for moving on without him; but that was unnecessary. His voice gave him away, and he was brought back to duty.

FORDING THE KIZIL-SU.

These Sarts are a cunning lot, and will take advantage wherever they can.   They are spending at least an hour fussing over their horses this morning, on the plea that the extra duration of yesterday's journey renders it necessary.   It makes no difference to me, as I shall insist upon just so many versts, no matter how late we are in getting off.   There is no use becoming impatient.   It simply starts them in a torrent of words, all of which are Greek to you, and also merely delays their progress.   You will have your way in the end; and if you have any serious trouble, simply threaten them with a report to the Russian governor of the province, and they will come down from their high positions at once.

"HOUTMART," July 12th.

That is as near to the name as I can make out from Rachmed's pronunciation.   It has no name or place on any map, but is simply two yourts that stand at the south of the Taldek Pass.   Here it was that B. and I separated a week ago, and here I am back again, en route to Europe, while he is lost somewhere in the snows to the southward. I am met and welcomed by several Kirghiz, who apologize for the absence of their Membashie. He has crossed the Taldek to meet General Jorneoff, who is en route to that much-watched region, the Pamirs. He is called their conqueror, though what satisfaction Russia has derived from the conquest of that region of snow and ice, a few wandering tribes and their flocks, remains to be seen. It certainly is of no use to the empire, and I do not think it ever can be. A jealous fear of England prompted the move. As I have stated before, I met this conqueror at dinner at the governor's house in Marghilan.

One soon learns to look upon a yourt as a place of refuge. Whenever I come across one at our resting places, I do not hesitate to enter, being sure of a welcome, unless some of the animals object. If they do, they are at once ejected.

July 14th.

To-day I bid farewell—and I suppose forever, as I shall not be likely to return here—to these

Alai Mountains.   They spread all along the south side of this great green valley in a wonderfully beautiful panorama.   There are four peaks in sight now that must certainly overtop any thing in Switzerland.   During the night fresh snow has fallen, and they glitter most dazzlingly down, almost to where the green line rises.   Beyond them lies the Pamirs, whither I should like to go if health permitted and I had a pleasant companion or two.   There is no use trying to go alone on such journeys.   Perhaps, if I had had companions, I might have done better this time; but no " company " can ward off bodily ills, though they may and do help one to bear them.

I shall anticipate here, and quote portions of a letter received from India.   It is dated the 2d of October, and is from Bylandt, showing that he has succeeded in making his tour, but that the journey was a hard one.

" I have had rather a hard time of it, but after all feel in capital spirits at having successfully accomplished even my dearest wish, namely, to cross Hunza.   I had to leave every thing and every body behind, and, all by myself, pushed on through the narrow gorges and along the rushing torrent of Hunza, with the roughest lot of coolies to carry my baggage. In the Tagh Dum Bash, two Chinese kept me a prisoner for three days. I succeeded in getting a good bag (ovis poli, bear, etc.). I am now trying to get my permission to find my way back through Afghanistan. If I should not succeed, I hope to go by Kelat and Persia. I am now on my way to Simla. I hope to look up Beddoes in Quetta, but have not yet found out whether he has returned to India. People are very kind to me. I am now staying with Baron Bentinck, a countryman of mine. Cashmere is a charming country. I stayed with the Resident in Srinagar. Your two countrymen, Church and Phillips, were very nearly starved to death on the Pamirs. Their coolies ran away, taking all their provisions. With best wishes for your entire recovery,

" Yours truly,

"J. DE BYLANDT."

I am indeed glad to know that he is safe, and sincerely trust that he has not been allowed to try the Afghan trip—one's life is not worth much in that country—though he will get through if any one can. He is most determined, and has both youth and perfect health on his side. It is and will always be a great regret to me that we separated, as I should, I feel convinced, have gotten on all right; and I mean to do that tour yet. However, in the safety and seclusion of one's own home, one resolves on many things that fate does not permit him to accomplish.

I awoke this morning and found the Sarts luxuriously asleep. One of them sent me word that he would go for the horses shortly. It is useless to say that he went very promptly. I have been rather too lenient with them. Like all servants over here, they respect only the hand that is firm. The "verst post," the first sign of civilization, has appeared again. As we slowly mount the approach to the Taldek Pass, I turn for a farewell view of the Alai. I shall always think of it as a place of green grass and many flowers, of gurgling brooks and snowy mountains; as a place where I have found true hospitality. My return passage of the " Taldek " is much more interesting than was the first, the scenery as viewed from the south being more rugged and bolder in outline. Of course, it in no way equals the view of the Trans-Ali, but you see none of that in your passage southward until the Taldek is far behind you. I am referring now simply to the scenery that pertains to that pass, and it is certainly much more interesting as viewed coming north. In addition, marvelous to relate, it does not in many places seem familiar, though my former passage was just ten days ago. So strange to me do portions of it appear, that I question Rachmed as to whether we have not come another route; but that could not be, as we are on the one military road in this section. The panorama is very varied and grand all day long, and the tempest of wind which sweeps from the north makes the day, which would otherwise be intensely hot, very pleasant. But it is all very solitary. Here and there one comes suddenly upon a lonely tomb. Each and all of the quaint structures have had their portals broken open by some marauder in search of treasure, which, of course, as the poor dead man had none in life, they find not.

We make forty-six versts to-day, and then halt on a green island in the Gulcha River. I immediately seek the shade of the adjacent cliffs, while Rachmed lies face down and goes to sleep with the sun blazing on his back. What a tough and what a queer people these Sarts are! Such an exposure would make a white man ill under this sun in short order. Just now, when I wanted to jump the stream, he objected, and wanted to carry me over. On my refusal, he went to sleep, while I sat down to watch for our caravan, which can not, on account of the passes and head winds, be here for an hour or so.

All along the route to-day we found yourts erected and peopled by the many Sart and Kirghiz dignitaries of the sections hereabouts, waiting for the passage of General Jorncoff, who, I hear, has reached Surfi-Kurghan. If so, we shall pass him to-morrow. One can easily see that, though young for a general, he is one of the strong arms of the great white Czar. His name, like all the other Russian names, I have given as it is pronounced. It would, in fact, be impossible to do otherwise.

I never stop for camp but that I am struck with the beauty of the flowers and vines. Around the basin of the brook yonder, they are arranged as though for a high festival; and are they not? Is not this the season of "high festival" in this land? and the beds of the rivers are the banquet halls. As I write, there are two impudent black birds with red beaks walking round and round my kodak, evidently regarding it with great curiosity. I wonder what they think of it. One has just given it a resounding whack with his beak, and both are now gone, in consequence of a rock sent at them in some irritation. Hunters are so few and far between that the game is very tame, though for that matter it is not tempting to shoot. I noticed some wild dogs this morning, and we are constantly barked at by the many marmots, which are almost too fat to waddle out of our way. Those, aside from a rabbit as big as a "Texas jack" and a solitary eagle, are all the game that I have seen. One must go to the Pamirs to find the Ovis Poli (mountain sheep) and other large game, and I am told that it is very scarce even there.

Rachmed has taken to opening my stores since my illness, and is greatly disgusted by my refusal to partake of such canned stuffs as they afford. But I dare not risk it; certainly not out here in the desert. He has just returned from a foraging expedition with a log of wood, and is delighted over the prospect of a somewhat better fire than dried manure generally affords. He tells me that, on his journey through Thibet with Orleans, nothing save manure could ever be found. That, thanks to the passage of the caravans of camels through the ages, was always plentiful. This is my last camp in the mountains of the Ali, though I left that region proper yesterday. To-day we halt at Gulcha, which is too low down to be called very mountainous. I shall lose also this delicious air, and shall

have to exist in the heat until I cross the
Caspian again.   I confess I dread the passage
of the "Sable Noir," but it will be made in
a good railway carriage, where I can take
proper care of myself.   One can not but feel
a regret that these rippling waters, that dance
so merrily onward, will find their end, not in
the ocean, but in the horrid sands of the Black
Desert, which all the waters of the globe could
not moisten or fertilize.

CHAPTER XVIII.

ABOUT an hour from camp we met the first of Jorneoff's forces—horses and donkeys, most of them, but each and all ladened with the necessaries for a three months' tour of the Pamirs. Then came the foot soldiers, about three hundred in all—Cossacks, of course—and a ragged, dirty-looking lot they were. No inspection in this department, or such uniforms would not be permitted. They are supposed to consist of black boots, red trousers, white jackets, and caps of linen; but to-day, including the faces and hair of the wearers, all were of a dust color, though there is comparatively no dust here. The men did not look simply travel-stained, as a marching army must, but were dirty with old dirt and grease. Passing General Jorneoff, I stopped for a moment's chat, and he kindly carried a letter to B., who, as he expects me in Srinagar, may as well be informed at

"Post Pamir" that I shall not reach there this time.

This Russian general's fame as conqueror of the Pamirs was acquired in a fashion scarcely to his credit. A small Afghan fort, on Afghan territory, guarded by a mere handful of soldiers, was summoned by him to surrender; which they very properly refused to do, stating that they were in their own fort and on their own territory, that they had been ordered to remain, and would be shot if they disobeyed the order. Jorneoff replied that they would be promptly shot if they did not, and slaughtered they were. The Russian force outnumbered the Afghans many times over, and it was a time of peace. So, at least, I am told from one who has many friends in St. Petersburg; and as I sat this morning on my horse and gazed into the cold, cruel-looking face of this commander so beloved by the government, I could well believe that he would allow nothing to stand long between himself and his advancement. His light blue eyes gleamed with a friendly glance on me, but cruelty, deep and awful, lay behind their smiles. I could not but wonder, as I watched him disappear up the defile, what record of blood—forever unknown to the world—will mark the passage of these bright summer months in the Pamirs. The shooting down of another handful of Afghans; perhaps the moving his soldiers rapidly from point to point of that desolate land, and the sending of high-sounding reports to the great white Czar, and receiving therefor further honors—greater rank? Very likely. In the meantime, what is Russia doing for the great cause of civilization and enlightenment in these provinces of Central Asia? And is it done for the benefit of the people, or the further glory of one man?

It is about twenty-five years since she laid her hand on this land of Turkistan, and it is now entirely possible to travel from end to end of it in safety, both as to life and property. Near each and every native town of any impor-tance she has built a Russian one, perfected irrigation, planted trees, caused the wilderness to "blossom like the rose." There are many schools, where the natives are taught the Russian tongue. She has built a railroad through the terrible " Black Sand Desert," to the gates of the city of Tamerlane, and is now surveying the route for its extension as far as Marghilan. When that is done, that picturesque terror, the " tarantass," will vanish into the remote regions between Marghilan and Gulcha, or, rather, between Marghilan and the other side of the Taldek Pass, over which there is a road now that could be easily made available for that national vehicle. At present, one must enter it at Samarkand, and five days later he will alight at "Osh" in fragments, having, during all the five hundred versts, envied that great two-wheeled cart, the "arba," as it rolled so smoothly though slowly along. My heavy tin boxes were split and cracked and polished clean of paint by the terrible motion, and my patience reduced to like condition through long delays at post-houses and indignation with stupid officials, said officials being all Russians, no Sarts holding offices of any description. In Osh, I watched with interest the high court of justice. To the presence of the governor the suppliants were ushered one by one. But short audiences were given to any of them; most were scarcely allowed to finish what they had to say; all were hustled away, generally carrying "No" as an answer to their petitions. I notice that in Russia "No" is the invariable answer to all things at *first*. You may, if sufficiently determined, cause it to be changed to "Yes," but at first you will receive a decided "No," no matter what you ask. It seems to be indicative of the character of the government—an absolute monarchy, where the people, be they of high or low rank, have no rights, where they have "no business to be asking questions," or wanting any thing that the Czar does not accord them unasked; and if they are discovered thinking, much less acting, for themselves, they know that it means Siberia. These Sarts are cheerful-natured, and take the ruling of their western masters in a most philosophical manner. I do not think one of the entire lot that day got what he wanted. Yet none seemed greatly to mind it, or perhaps they have early learned the uselessness of opposition. Russia has them by the neck, and forces them to live at peace with the world and each other. But does she do so for their own good; does she hold any good feeling toward them, or toward any other of her conquered provinces? Is it not simply for the greater military glory of the "Czar?" For the "Czar" is Russia and Russia is the "Czar"—all the other seventy millions of human beings are mere ciphers, though this is the nineteenth century. Look at the treatment of Poland. It will answer the question I have asked. Austria and Germany make but little difference in the government of their portions of that dismembered kingdom from that which they accord to other sections of their county. But with Russia! If a man is a Pole, he is accorded much the same treatment that "Jean val Jean," in Hugo's great work, received from the police of France. I know of a case in point to-day, where Russia has received twenty years of faithful service from a Pole, who is as loyal to the Czar as any native born Russian; and yet, though the best years of his life have been passed in faithful service to the crown, he can never reach the rank of general, but must stand aside and watch men far his inferior in every respect promoted over his head—and all because he is "a Pole!" So, to my thinking, it is and will be in Turkistan. Her people will be forever made to feel that they are conquered. The very arrangement of the cities must impress that fact upon the natives. At each and all of the great points and larger towns, the native portions are entirely to themselves, communicating in no way with the Russian portion, and ofttimes, as in the case of Bokhara, Tashkend, and Marghilan, three, four, and even ten miles separate them. The Russian towns are nothing save military posts, always heavily armed and always on guard, and it is utterly impossible that the people of Turkistan should, under such circumstances, feel otherwise than that they are treated as though in a vast prison. Such may be, in a measure, necessary with these tribes, but such is the case throughout all the vast extent of Russia's empire, be it civilized or savage. To these distant provinces the Czar sends also, sometimes for life, those of his nobles or his relatives who have displeased him, and whom he does not desire to brand as convicts by sending to Siberia. Tashkend is full of such, and is called the capital of the banished.

But, for the matter of that, it is not so much better for a native born Russian. He will, it is true, receive advancement before all others, up to a certain point; but each rank cowers before the one above it, and all tremble before the Czar; and by the "Czar" I do not mean the man, but the office, to which Alexander III is as great a slave as any of his empire. Seventy millions of automatons, who think and move, and have almost their being, through the will of one man. What comparisons one of another nation—knowing India—is forced to make as he journeys through Turkistan! True, it is, perhaps, unfair to make such comparison where the one nation has held control for more than a century and the other not one-fourth so long;

but remember Poland, and judge the future for Turkistan by Poland's past. The world will never be shocked by such tales of cruelty in the case of the Asiatic country, because she is Asiatic and will stand more oppression.

What would be the condition of India at present had she—in 1857—been under the dominion of Russia and risen in mutiny against the Czar? Would you find, as does the traveler of to-day in that land of the sun, every office in the hands of the people that can be placed there? Would you, entering the great banks, railway offices, custom houses, etc., find them, as you now do, all in native hands? Would you find regiment after regiment of native soldiers? Would you find any one save Russians, Russians, Russians, with the people of the land crushed down and out of sight? Even the terrible mutiny only caused England to give the people more liberty. Would it have been so under Russia? Russia feels very bitterly about the articles that have appeared concerning her in the press of the world—notably those by Kennan, because they come from an American. She has always been most friendly toward that people, and I fancy that "America" is most friendly toward her; but until she wheels into line with the other great nations of the earth in the matter of progress and enlightenment, until she leaves the midnight of the sixteenth century for the daylight of this nineteenth, she can not expect the enlightened nations of the earth to hold great sympathy for her, much less that western land, which for one of its mottoes takes those immortal words, " with the people, by the people, and for the people."

Jorneoff's baggage train was immense, and I warrant that he travels with all luxury. No simple rice night after night, because he can not eat mutton eternally. Nor would there have been for me, had I in any way understood the resources, or lack thereof, of the land. On another trip things would be very different. I have roughed it for weeks in our Rockies and elsewhere, and certainly think I can get on with as little as most men; but there are few who can exist, as the Kirghiz do, on tea and tough mutton. In our mountains, one always has fresh game of some sort, and I warrant there is not a ranch in the whole land but can give you one ham at all times, to say nothing of the other meats. With those things properly cooked—and what guide at home can not cook?—one can get on very well. But after a long and hot day's ride, to know that nothing save the eternal mutton and tea await one, is more than most well men can endure for a protracted period. You will ask why I do not use the stores I possess. I do so wherever I can, but what are they? A bag of Sart bread that an ax will not cut, and which must be soaked in hot water in order to be used at all—yet it is all that you can procure, and you must bring that from Osh; then some boxes of semi-sweet crackers, a cake of soup, some gingersnaps, a few cans of sardines and venison—all of which are most ancient, to say the least. You can also purchase chocolates and sweetmeats, but one can not live on such things.

While I am on this subject, it would perhaps be well to give a word of advise to those who may follow, and also a short explanation of the tours. As for the season, one should leave Osh not later than June 1st. That will make the journey over the desert quite pleasant. I do not consider a journey to St. Petersburg as at all necessary. If you go to Odessa and send your passports to the capital, our minister can do it all without your aid. Then, when you are assured that your permission has been granted, telegraph yourself to the governor of Askhabad, and ask whether you will be permitted to enter at Usin-ada. Remember the three Americans who were turned back this year, notwithstanding their permission. Pay three prices for your telegram, and also for the response. In such cases your message is given precedence over all others, and you will receive your reply in a few hours. If it is favorable, then go ahead; and if the police at Usin-ada refuse you an entrance, just show that telegram, as I did, and demand that they wire at once to Askhabad. That will force their hands. They are simply trying to bluff you, as they did in my case. You have all day in which to do this. Once on the train, there will be no more trouble; and if you take the precaution to procure some letters of introduction (and even if not), you will be treated with a hospitality—by the powers that rule—to which you are unaccustomed at home, no matter where you live. I do not mean in splendor—Turkistan is too remote for that—but, a hospitality in which one feels that with the bread and salt is also given a true and warm welcome. Witness that extended to B. and myself, who certainly had no claim upon him, by Colonel Grombschefsky at Osh. He was indeed a good Samaritan, and I have no doubt, when I reach there again day after to-morrow, but that his hand, his heart, and his table will be open and at my service. So much for getting into the land. Now for the route.

The most direct is *via* Odessa, Batoum, and Baku, unless one happens to be in St. Petersburg, when the shorter route is *via* Petrovsky and thence to Usin-ada. Your provisions and luggage for Turkistan can be sent by sea direct from New York to Batoum, and I strongly recommend a supply of the former from Park & Tilford's. There is a peculiar prejudice against all canned goods in Russia, and you will find, unless you take them with you, which will cost but little, that you will suffer from the lack thereof. I do not mean luxuries or fancy articles, but vegetables, and all good canned meats, fish, cured hams and tongues; also canned fruits. You can get none of these in Turkistan. We did find a few cans of salmon and venison, but of inferior make, often spoiled, always greasy. In the mountains and on the plains, you will find absolutely nothing save mutton and tea. As for clothing, you will need both light and heavy. If you go to the Pamirs, a fur-lined overcoat suitable for the purpose can be purchased very cheaply at Osh; and at Samarkand, all the blankets and heavy covering one may need. There is no trouble about the very necessary cognac until you reach Kashgar. It is always on hand in every Russian town. Of course, if you are going on such a tour as our countrymen from St. Louis made on their bicycles, you can take nothing, and must put up with what the countries afford; but I see no merit in depriving oneself of the necessities of life when there is absolutely no need for so doing, and when they can be carried so cheaply.

CHAPTER XIX.

LANGAR.

AT Akbosoga, I learn to my sorrow that Colonel Grombschefsky is en route to the mountains to inspect the roads, etc. This is bad news for me, as Osh is nothing without him. I had looked forward to the meeting with much pleasure, but as matters turned out, was not doomed to entire disappointment. As I descended the last pass to this place, Langar, I found him asleep in his yourt, and his numerous attendants occupied in like manner outside. He did what he could, and it was a great deal, to make my visit to Osh pleasant. He sent me direct to the "Club," so that a repetition of that post-house visit was avoided.

I can not but wish that Colonel Grombschefsky was giving the best years of his life to some other government. I discovered, though not from himself, that he is a Pole. He is one of the finest specimens of manhood and of a soldier that I have ever met with, and is faithful to Russia in every thought and feeling, and would add luster to her name of an enduring quality. Russia does not deserve the loyalty of his silence. I bade him farewell with regret, and turned again and again to wave an adieu and watch his white coat as it vanished into a mere speck in the distant landscape. What does he think of it himself, I wonder. The best years of his life to a government that will never reward him, that has kept him forever exiled to this remote land, that will promptly forget him once his usefulness is gone! Like a sucked orange, he will be tossed into a corner—" only a Pole!"

I learn that the Czar would greatly like to visit Turkistan, but that, as his visit would cost some two million roubles, he dare not squander that amount.

Upon arrival at Osh, I found comfortable quarters at the Club, but the emptiness and loneliness thereof was something appalling. Numbers of rooms, saloons, billiard and dancing halls, and a theater, but no one to occupy them

save myself and one officer, who sleeps all
day. The town is as lonely as the Club.
You may walk her streets for hours and see
no one save some pale-faced women staring at
you through the dusty panes of some window.
I find even my fat hostess at the post-house
has vanished—"been turned out." So I make
speed to get away eastward, though it is with
great regret that I leave the cool winds of the
mountains for the hot plains below. Our tarantass we sold, and it has been resold and is
gone; so I am forced to take one from the
post as far as Marghilan, one hundred versts.
The vehicle is horrible and the ride appalling.
The less said about it the better.

At Marghilan, I met a different sort of
Russian from Colonel Grombschefsky—in fact,
one of the usual sort; one who insisted that
I use his tarantass and not buy one, that I
would be given special permission for horses,
etc. I was quite overwhelmed and knew not
how to express my thanks, especially for the
latter, considering my weak condition. I might
have saved myself any surplus of gratitude. In

less than an hour he arrived at my hotel and withdrew every thing. "His wife had promised the tarantass;" specials "were not necessary." In other words, like most of his nation, he was all promise and no performance—lip service. I speedily secured the services of the hotel keeper and started out to buy a tarantass, which I succeeded in doing very shortly. Of course, the Sart, knowing my necessity, made me pay for it, but the very high charge of seventy-five roubles ($37.50) had to be endured. Two hours were needed to put it in condition, but by 5 P. M. I was rattling through the streets of Marghilan, having bade farewell to the little policeman who spoke such good English and desired so greatly to come with me. Early in life he had ran away to sea, and, landing in Halifax, learned our tongue, a fact which makes him constantly an object of suspicion to his governor. I telegraphed to this governor of Marghilan from Osh, asking if I might take the youth through to Srinagar with me. The result was, to me, a curt refusal, and to him, a threatened arrest. Why, is more than I can tell. So he can not come now, and watches me wistfully as I roll away to the outer world, to that freedom whose very meaning is unknown in Russia.

July 19th.

Two stages of thirty-two versts only, and I stick for nine hours, because there are no horses. So I settle in my tarantass and am soon deep in slumber. It is raining this morning, a thing almost unknown in Turkistan in summer. I have been singularly fortunate in the matter of weather. It has been cool and cloudy, and if this continues I shall not have a hard ride over the numerous deserts between here and the Caspian Sea.

Kojend, July 21st.

The good weather, *i. e.*, clouds and showers, is still with me. All day yesterday was cloudy, with light showers, which at night increased to a heavy rain, and by midnight, when we reached Kojend, its downpour was so steady that I was forced, on Rachmed's account—he rides outside—to lay over for four hours. To-day opens cloudy, and this usual furnace is cool and pleasant. The entire ride from Kojend to Jisak is a pleasant one, and very far more interesting than that *via* Tashkend. One is on the first rise of the mountains all the way, and thereby avoids the desert entirely.

Good luck in the matter of weather deserts us at Jisak. We reach there at 4 P. M., only to find every thing held in abeyance for the passage of the post. I wish I could in any way or degree make you understand the terrible filth and dirt of these Turkistan post-houses. This one at Jisak rivals the others. Imagine an inclosure of mud walls some hundreds of feet in extent, on one side the stalls, on the other the post-house, which is generally a low, white structure, full of filth and flies. The square itself is a mass of accumulated manure, bits of harness, broken-down tarantasses, mangy dogs, and what appear to be bundles of rags, that may at one time have served as bedding. Nothing human in sight at first, but a vigorous calling evolves these bundles of rags into men and women and many children. Out of one of them comes the postman and his wife, not so much ragged as utterly vile with old filth. They have simply brought out an old comforter, and, dropping it any place, on filth or otherwise, gone sound asleep. As to intellect, they are but little above the dogs that sleep on top of them. It would not be possible for such a state of degradation to be found in our country, even amongst the lowest negroes. In the midst of such vileness we were forced to wait for hours. I tried my best to bribe the postman—even got him gloriously drunk, he and a crazy Jew merchant, who tried to make me drink his tea—but all to no effect. It was five hours before we got off, only to be shortly enveloped in such clouds of dust that my driver was forced to slow up now and then, like a ship in a fog.

Shortly after leaving Jisak, the road enters the narrow defile of Jitan-uti, supposed to be greatly infested with serpents. Through it, in days of old, the hordes of Mongol and Turkish savages obtained access to the fertile valley of the Zarafshan; and high on the right, where the defile is narrowed, one sees the so-called Tablets of Tamerlane, though neither of them bears the name of that conqueror. One is

A FUTURE POST DRIVER.

shaped like an old-fashioned headstone, round at the top, while the other is square. The inscriptions are in Persian, and state that:

"With the help of God the Lord, the great Sultan, conqueror of kings and nations, shadow of God on earth, the support of the decisions of the *Sunna* and of the divine law, the ruler and aid of the faith, Ulug Bek Gurugan—may God prolong the time of his reign and rule!—undertook a campaign into the country of the Mongols, and returned from this nation and these countries uninjured, in the year 828 (A. D. 1425)."

The Ulug Bek mentioned was grandson to Tamerlane, and the founder of Samarkand's observatories and colleges. The second inscription is of the victory of Abdullah Khan, a century and a half later: "Let passers in the waste and travelers on land and water know, that in the year 979 (A. D. 1571), there was a conflict between the army of the lieutenant of the Khalefate, the shadow of the Almighty, the great Khakan Abdullah Khan, son of Iskinder Khan, consisting of thirty thousand men of war, and the army of Dervish Khan and Baba Khan and other sons of Barak Khan. In this army there were fifty relatives of the Sultan and four hundred thousand fighting men from Turkistan, Tashkend, Ferghana, and Deshia Keptchak. The army of the Sovereign, by the fortunate conjunction of the stars, gained the victory, having conquered the above mentioned Sultans, and gave to death so many of them that, from the people who were killed in the fight and after being taken prisoners, during the course of one month, blood ran on the surface of this river to Jizakh. Let this be known."

One can not but feel that all that had and still has something to do with the present filth of Jisak; and I do not altogether object to these clouds of dust, as they shut out my last view of the filthy place. The native tribes of these eastern countries are dirty enough, but plant amongst them a low type of our much-vaunted civilization, and it will soon outdo the sons of the soil in the matter of filth. It may, perhaps, seem worse in the Europeans, because, knowing that they know better, we therefore expect more of them. At all events, I should prefer to pass the night in an Arab khan to spending it as they do, down in the filth of a stable-yard. Let us leave them. Even as I write, the dust lifts, and the snowy peaks beyond Samarkand sparkle in the sunlight. There, I know, are green trees, rushing waters, eternal freshness—thanks to the gold of the Zarafshan. There, also, is the conceited little post-master, who takes such an interest in my mails that I know I only receive about half that arrive. There, again, I shall hear English, when I meet the good M. Letellier (though it will be funny English). There, are some Russians who were very good to us on our way out. There I shall find Madam Metzler; and last, but not least, in her comfortable "inn," shall find a "warmest welcome" in a hot bath. Have you ever traveled day and night for a week in a tarantass? Have you ever been forced to make examination as to whether or not your bones were coming through your corduroys? If not, you can in no way understand the delight that latter prospect was to me, emerging from such a ride. Still, one learns to adapt oneself to every situation, and I have slept soundly many nights, while my horses plunged wildly onward over these deserts, rocking and swaying my vehicle until, had I not been deeply imbedded therein, I should certainly have been thrown out. I awoke last night—it was bright moonlight—to find the horses apparently running away, and Rachmed violently belaboring the driver. Without waiting to inquire into the cause, I joined him in his work. He shook and I pummeled, with my cap, the stolid coachman, who held firmly to his lines and appeared to mind us not one whit. Rachmed gasped out, between attacks: "We are lost! lost!" Those were the Famished Steppes, where next day the heat would mount to one hundred and thirty and upward! What were we to do? Away on all sides stretched the dead level. Over its surface the moonlight played strange pranks, with sage bushes withered and skeleton-like through the awful heat by day. Solitary turtles made stately progress, like huge black roaches, toward the horizon. The misty shadows chased each other like Tam O'Shanter's witches, and over all and through all there was such dead silence. Rachmed went

off with the driver and one horse to search for
the road, and I, alone in the tarantass in the
midst of that desolation, wondered what the
outcome would be, and wondering, passed into
dreamland, where I was soon surrounded by the
phantom men and beasts, wolves and savages
that have swept those plains for centuries, and
with all of whom Rachmed seemed fighting in
my defense. Then I awoke at Jisak, and the
morning of my last day's ride in a tarantass.

Later in the day, the road became so rough
that twice the tarantass broke down. Finally,
when I thought, on seeing the last post before
Samarkand, come into view, that our woes were
over, I found such a crowd of waiting tarantasses that all hope of progress for at least
twenty-four hours was gone. It was simply
impossible to stay there. There was not even
a dirty spot on which to sit down, and absolutely
no chance of any thing to eat. Summoning
Rachmed, I told him to get a horse at any
price, and I would ride into Samarkand, and he
could follow when he could. He succeeded in
his quest, and I shortly found myself en route,

in company with some dozens of Sarts, each and every one of whom considered it his special duty to see that I got on all right. When the Zarafshan River was reached, they would have insisted that I dismount and enter one of the great, lumbering arbas for the passage; but, shaking them off, I pushed on and made the passage ahead of the lot, which secured me their intense admiration. It was nearly nine o'clock when I dismounted at Hotel Metzler, where I found a welcome, bed, bath, and dinner, and which five nights in my tarantass enabled me to fully appreciate. As for the clothing that I stripped off that night, from hat to shoes, I never saw it again. My vehicle arrived, in charge of Rachmed, before 10 A. M., and in a short time I was offered twenty roubles for it. It cost seventy-five. I declined the offer, and left it in Madam's hands, to be disposed of as she thought best. I have just heard (September) that it is still "for sale," and will be until I return to Central Asia, I fancy.

Samarkand was very attractive, and I was greatly tempted to linger. It was cool and delightful, and the fruits were at their best. I never saw finer melons, grapes, apricots, apples, plums, or peaches; and I fancy, from what I hear, that though Turkistan may fail in many ways, she more than holds her own in regard to fruit. But all the fruit in the Garden of Eden could not have kept me from a start homeward in the train that left at 8 P. M., especially as I found I would have an American for a companion as far as Askhabad. Even the prospect of great heat in the desert was ignored, and I started once more westward. Madam again was "*désolé*," and gave me two small chickens as a parting gift. Rachmed did not demand more than his wages, and seemed deeply grateful for the small present I gave him. I also gave him a note of commendation, but said very little therein, simply stating that he was sober, honest, and faithful; and that he was a good guide in every sense of the word. I would not say that I thought he was stupid, as those who will employ him will discover. He has been made intensely conceited by having been brought so prominently before the world in his trips with famous people, and charges for said fame. I paid him one hundred and twenty-five roubles per month, which was double his worth. He would be a good under-servant in a camp, but that is all; and he seems to possess absolutely no memory—your orders must be reiterated each day. But enough of Rachmed. He was very kind during my illness, and for that I am deeply grateful.

CHAPTER XX.

July 24th.

ANY thing that moves by steam is marvelous to one after the slower tarantass; and how luxuriously smooth and comfortable these old, worn-out carriages appear! What a superb affair that whitewashed freight car that does duty as a dining car! One could travel to Cape Horn with such comforts. Surely, all things are comparative; at least it would seem so here, as I look back at my first impression of this same train. It is cool enough at night, and, though in our passage of the desert the thermometer mounts, in the car, to one hundred and ten (Fahr.), I do not feel it nearly so much as I have done eighty or ninety on a murky day at home, so perfectly dry and healthy is the air.

On the evening of the second day, we pass the ruins of ancient Merve, sharply and fantastically outlined against the "crimson glow of evening."

Merve was old in the days of Darius. She was a colony of Alexander and a Parthian province. Also a Christian bishopric in A. D. 200. Here the veiled prophet of Khorasan kindled the fumes of schism in the eighth century. Jenghiz Khan passed through it like a flaming sword, and Russia wiped it from the face of the earth.

Old Merve has been thrice destroyed by conquering armies, but has never, as I was erroneously informed, been buried in the sand. It is clear of sand now. New Merve is an hour away by train and on the river. I notice many of those quaint-looking little towers of defense here and there over the desert. Built of mud, they are high enough to hold a man standing upright, and have no entrance save a hole near the base, through which the occupant crawls. He is supplied with rocks inside to close the entrance, and for use as weapons, and when once inside is comparatively safe, as the sun turns the mud almost to stone. These plains of Turkistan are dotted with ruined cities. We are passing another, quite as extensive as old

Merve, and with several very stately mosques rising above the general ruin.

Askhabad is reached at noon the second day, and here I lose my companion. Around the place will forever hang the memory of that terrible visitation of cholera, three years since. Some of the scenes, though terrible, were romantic, and one could have been taken as the original of Poe's "Mask of the Red Death." The pestilence was supposed to have passed on its way, after leaving its five thousand dead. General Kuropatkine, in very desperation at the terrible gloom, concluded to give a banquet. Gay was the event, but before another sun had set nearly every soul who had attended was dead. The cholera had returned, and each and all, from the highest guest to the most humble musician, had bowed before its awful presence.

Askhabad is a modern Russian town of no special interest, but I notice some miles to the eastward an entire city, walled and almost perfect, but silent and deserted. Above it rise the arches of a great ruined mosque, but human life has left it long ago.

It is with a feeling of great relief that I catch sight of the first waters of the Caspian, and the little ship that receives me at Usin-ada seems a haven of rest. Usin-ada is situated in an arm of the Black Desert, which here stretches its claws outward toward the sea itself. They say that Russia has plans for a vast scheme, if she ever has the money therefor. She hopes, by the union of two rivers to the north of the Caucasus, to unite the Black Sea and the Caspian, and, as the latter is eighty-five feet lower than the former, to introduce such floods of water that all the Caspian and the region round about will be covered by the excess thereof, and which must steadily rise until the level of the Black Sea be reached. Where are now useless deserts will then be a vast inland sea, which will change the entire climate of Turkistan, enabling the people to raise vast quantities of cotton, and so shut out our markets, etc. But Russia has not the money, even if it could be done; and I think it is all talk, as by such a change the entire oil regions would be destroyed, and the empire lose the source of its greatest wealth. Therefore, Turkistan will remain a vast desert, backed by a towering range of mountains; in the former, a few oases, where a man may live; in the latter, a high, cold valley, accessible only for the brief summer months; the whole governed by a power that does all for the glory of the Czar, and little for the advancement of the people.

And so, as I watch the yellow shores of Turkistan sink below the level of the blue Caspian, I can not but feel that her future is a very dark one so long as she is ruled over by the great white Czar; and by the " Czar " I mean the office,' not the man. Alexander, like all his predecessors of this century, is a man of advanced ideas, though he is not an intellectual man; but he is bound as in bands of steel by the traditions of the empire.

As I look back over the tour, it has been a satisfactory one, notwithstanding the great disappointment of not getting through to Cashmere. However, I have seen the best at this end, and shall see the other at some future day. As for Kashgar, Yarkand, and the Devil Desert which joins them, I feel no regret at missing, nor shall I ever attempt to see them. They are simply two more Sart towns, and not Chinese at all, and of Sart towns I have had my fill. To Samarkand I award the prize for interest and beauty above all others. It alone possesses extensive remains of the past. Its climate is fine, and there is a charm peculiarly its own which one can not describe. Tashkend is devoid of interest, save as the military head-quarters. If you prize "a dinner with the governor-general," you must go there to get it. I do not. As to Bokhara, it is interesting as your first Sart city. Its mosque is unique. I have been asked whether I did not consider that it possessed a "cachet" of its own. No; most certainly I did not. It is greatly like the inferior portions of many other oriental cities, and Sart Tashkend and Kokand, though smaller, are greatly like it. Osh is a beautiful hamlet in the mountains. So much for the works of man. For those of the Great

Creator, what can one say? They are grand and full of interest, though, as in the case of the "Sable Noir," they are at times terrible. Yet that same desert was most fascinating, and I never tired looking at its fantastic shapes and forms, at its ever changing waves of sand, while I appreciated the fact that to be out there for an hour would have meant death. When one comes to the Alai Mountains, there is little to say, because no words will do them justice. Having once entered that enchanted region, the memory of its snows and rippling waters, its deep green grasses, its rocks spangled with "edle-weiss" and "forget-me-nots," its pastoral life, its peace with all, will come to you again and again like "thoughts in a dream."

If the time ever comes when Russia awakes to a nineteenth century state of affairs, when one can visit all this without the slow desert journey and the horrors of a tarantass, then Turkistan will become for the world a great resort; but now Russia does not want you, and the inconveniences of travel are very great.

I have just learned that, at that famous

banquet at Askhabad, given by General Kuropatkine in honor of the emperor's birthday, between five and six hundred soldiers died of the cholera; and when I asked what he meant by giving a banquet at such a time of horror, I was met with a blank stare of surprise and the reply: "It was the emperor's birthday." Perish the world, but celebrate the emperor's birthday!

The passage of the Caspian comes like a pause in strife. Cool, calm, and beautiful, one enjoys every moment. The tour has been a long one, covering some ten thousand miles in three months, but is nearly over now.

Again ancient, oily Baku opens its ports to receive me, and there I am forced to pass a long, hot day, as the train does not leave until 11 P. M. The heat, because of its humidity, seems more unbearable than that of Turkistan. During the six hundred miles of railway ride between Baku and Batoum, I am about devoured by mosquitoes, and quite ready to plunge into the Black Sea when its dancing waters come in sight.

ANCIENT BAKU.

Batoum nestles in a nook in the mountains, but it is not a point of any interest; and as I find a Messargerie boat leaving within a few hours of my arrival, I am soon gliding over " the dancing waters of the deep blue sea." It is with a feeling of happiness that I see the last Russian vanish over the side of the ship. The constant espionage and restraint has been very galling. They have been very polite about it, but it was there all the same, and the knowledge riled one. Here you must obtain permission to depart. His majesty was loth to receive me, and now seems as loth to let me go. My desire to slap the smiling, hypocritical face of the man who demanded my passport was only restrained by the knowledge that I was still within their boundaries, though on a French ship. But the numerous visás, all of them so much more powerful than any he could give, caused that official to restore the paper with a deep salutation and a backing out of my presence.

Here we receive the news of the earthquake at Constantinople, of the Chicago riots, and of the late terrible accident to a Russian ship on these waters.

The character of the power of the Czar was to me never more fully illustrated than in the utter ignorance and indifference of the Russians to what goes on in the great world. When I questioned one, he replied: " What difference do the things of the outer world make to us? What are they to us? We may feel sorry that Madam Carnot has lost her husband, if we think of it at all, but that is all. Why should we care what goes on in France?" A veritable wall built around seventy millions of human beings by the power of one man! I had always imagined that state of affairs was con-fined to the ignorant classes; but it extends to all ranks, and if to-morrow they were or-dered to march, they would move onward, unthinking, unknowing, and uncaring; move forward as does an engine when the lever is pulled. But under all this there does exist a feeling of rebellion against this body and soul enchainment, and through the hearts of thousands pass thoughts and hopes of, as one told me not long since, a "war in Europe, in order that revolution may raise its head again in Russia," and that thereby this "suffocating blanket of oppression pass away forever." They all know of Kennan and his terrible articles. If you question a Russian officer, possessing power and loving it, he will at once denounce the whole as "lies," and then he will watch you out of the corner of his eye to see whether he has been able to deceive you. But if you happen to meet a student from Moscow, as I did, he will tell you that they are all true, and the half has not yet been told. I have left Russia and her sealed provinces. From many of her people I have received the marks of the greatest friendship and attention, without which I could not have gotten on; and to those I shall ever turn again and again, as the years glide onward, with pleasant thoughts and well wishes. That the traveler has not been able to write more favorably of their form of government, is because he comes from a progressive and enlightened people, and can, therefore, in no way understand or tolerate a nation of so many millions that, in this nine-teenth century, will contentedly remain in the darkness of the Middle Ages.

Of Russia as a great power, I have not much idea. I do not think she is strong. True, she possesses a great army, but it is, in proportion to her needs and her country to be defended, no larger than ours, of which we certainly do not boast. To guard Russia proper from Turkey, from Germany, and from England, would alone take all her army, leaving the whole of Turkistan open to invasion from England on the Indian side, from China to the eastward, and to internal rebellion, rapine, and murder. As for her Siberian possessions, she could not possibly protect them; but she is probably aware that their best protection lies in their terrible climate and in the fact that no one would have them as a gift. A war would also mean revolution internal in Russia, and what the result would be for her is plainly to be seen. She has sowed the wind; she will most certainly reap the whirlwind. The shadows of night gather thick and dark over her possession in this sea as the ship sails outward, and soon Batoum is but a serpent of glimmering lights against the towering mountains, and then vanishes in the sea.

"GOOD-NIGHT."

CHAPTER XXI.

TREBIZOND, July 29th.

A WILD babel of voices awakens me long before I desire it, and I lie for awhile wondering where I am and what it means. Certainly the gang outside are not Russians, and are not afraid of expressing their opinions in, I should judge, fifty different languages. What a pretty picture! Over the surface of the bright green water dozens of brilliantly painted boats glide hither and thither, each crowded with fantastically dressed boatmen and merchants, with baskets of fruit, etc. Beyond, on a sloping shore, rises the old city of Trebizond. Its gaily painted houses are deeply embowered in stately cypress trees, while far above all the green hills slumber in the morning light. After such a spot as Usin-ada, Trebizond, from the sea, is most picturesque, though internally she is not very interesting. We are here but a few hours, sailing westward with the sunset.

The southern shores of the Black Sea are dotted their entire length with attractive-looking places. The towns appear prosperous, the land has a cultivated look, and although all is under the rule of the heathen Turk, it presents an appearance of happiness not to be met with in the dominions of Russia, and, in fact, reminds one very much of the Riviera.

Later in the day, we pause for an hour or so. The usual mountains, with a village scattered over their side and ending in a ruined castle on a hill; the usual bright blue waters, brilliantly painted boats, jargon of tongues, and jumble of colors. That is Terresco. Feeling sure that distance lends enchantment to the view, we do not go ashore. The day is too warm to justify much exercise. So I spend the time hanging over the ship's rail, trying to excite a score or more of boatmen to renewed quarrels. Judging by the noise, I am somewhat successful. How little things change in this part of the world! Here comes a boat ladened with water jars, just such as were used at the " marriage in Cana." A lot of old

Turks have come on board, and are sitting in solemn, silent rows. No one has spoken to them, nor do they speak to each other. After awhile, in the same solemn silence, they depart. It is excitement for them, as, of course, with the absolute seclusion of their women, such a thing as society can not exist at home. They will go back to the dead silence of their houses, varied only occasionally by the senseless chatter of the women, quarreling probably about their last box of sweetmeats. There is here an effort to change the usual order of things. From the center of the town rises a great, new, white school-house. But I fancy the apparent prosperity is all sham, as are most other things under the dominion of the Sultan.

SINOPE, July 30th.

This is a day that one must "kill." We hold an absolutely clean bill of health, but, notwithstanding, here we must anchor for twenty-four hours; that it is not much longer we may be thankful for. This is a sheltered bay, to the north of which projects a long peninsula, and on that are a dozen or more detached houses—pest-houses. Where the peninsula joins the mainland rises a massive fortress, so that, once encaged on that bit of land yonder, there is no escape, save by water. It is a far better station than New York possesses for her quarantine, and is heaven itself in comparison to any in Spain, or even at Marseilles. The wind to-day is cool and strong, and comes ladened with salt from the sea. The day will be a weary one, but there are always letters to write, and one can spend much time at the table. We have endeavored to bribe the port physician with champagne to shorten our probation—but to no effect—" twenty-four hours." I think, perhaps, when I reach Vienna, I shall be quarantined because of the earthquakes at Constantinople. We are boarded by two villainous-looking " guardians of the public health," that appear as though they carried on their vile persons all the concentrated epidemics that have passed this way for years back. Our " steerage" is hustled ashore first, and we go later on. The lazarettos are comfortable frame houses, containing two rooms, each about fifteen feet square. The one we enter certainly is very clean, and, with comfortable beds, would not be a bad abiding place if one were quarantined here; but it gives us an uncomfortable sensation to smell iodoform and chloride of lime over all, and to notice that even the grass has been burned. There has been no epidemic this year—only some sporadic cases, of which there are one or two here now. Viewed from these windows, our ship floats a very emblem of liberty, a very portal of Heaven. After all, the fumigation is much of a farce, so far as we are concerned. I most certainly could carry away no end of bacilli. The ceremony over, I wander to the cliff's side and watch our boatmen in the waters below. What superb forms! They put to shame the Apollo. How entirely impossible such evenly perfect development is with artificial training! They make me wish I had been raised more like a duck or a water-dog. I doubt if I would have been obliged to turn back from the Chinese desert had such been the case. But these men are mere animals after all; so things are not so unevenly distributed. We are not long in taking to our boat, and are soon once again on the ship, feeling sure that, when she moves, we shall not be left behind. The two other vessels near us both spent a month here last year, at which time some four hundred persons died at this station alone. Situated as it is at the center of the southern coast, it is the grand depot for all this section. A Turkish ship is here for a week even now, her cook having succumbed to the pest. Of course, no intercourse is permitted with either of them, and, in fact, they look as though they were deserted. It is all very depressing, and one hurries the day along as something to be done with and forgotten. Yet I have no doubt that those who were cast here during last year's epidemic met with much more hospitable treatment than was accorded the passengers on the "Normannia," in the same year, at Fire Island.

One comes upon queer scenes in these eastern ships. It is about 10 P. M., and very dark outside. I wander out onto the lower deck for a breath of air before turning in, when I am attracted by the sound of a voice in recitation, evidently a cultivated voice. I might from here think I am listening to Coquelin Cadet, and that is one of Hugo's trage-dies. Going nearer, I discover the reciter to be one of the ship's stokers. Naked to the waist, black and grimy, he stands there a perfect Vulcan, while the stanzas roll from his throat in majestic music. His auditors, some naked and dirty like himself, and others, stolid-faced Turks and Armenians, form a semi-circle around him—invisible all, save when some passenger strikes a match, or the light from below glares for a moment. Out in the darkness gleam the lights of the pest ships and the pest town, while overhead the stars shine brilliantly. How impossible to find in Russia a man in his position with his mind and education! How different his quick, bright glance and rapid gestures (when the darkness permits one to see them) from the stupid, stolid, sodden faces in his rank in the Holy

Empire! The two types make one thoroughly understand why revolution has failed in Russia and been so successful in France; and just so long as Russia can keep up her stupefying, deadening policy, she will retain her absolute hold over her people. But when that slumbering volcano—an oppressed and outraged people—breaks its crust, that old revolution in France will have been as child's play by comparison. As I close my "port." for the night, I hear the same voice chanting the prayer from "Moses in Egypt." He is only a stoker, but he is at no man's beck and call. He has time to sing, he has the heart to sing, for his life is his own.

Before leaving quarantine this morning, we were greeted by the news that cholera is epidemic in St. Petersburg, and has also appeared at Adrianople. That shuts me out of the latter place, which I had hoped to visit. We live in hopes that the pest will delay its appearance at Constantinople until after our arrival, which, if all goes well, should take place to-morrow noon. That it will appear there I have not much doubt. The late earthquake, with its trail of dead, must certainly further that appearance. I learned in Osh that the black plague always exists in many of the cities of Western China, which rather lessens my desire for oriental investigation at those points. It would seem that no epidemic could long exist in the glorious air that sweeps around this ship to-day.

The Bosphorus is almost in sight, but we must stop an hour for medical inspection. It means nothing, but the news that may reach us means much. Those in security have no idea what a quarantine at Constantinople would be. One would not only be subjected to it there, but wherever one might happen to go thereafter, until Northern Europe be reached. That might take two months and more. I might go on in this ship and risk quarantine at Marseilles, but I think I should prefer to land here. Marseilles itself is one of those pest spots that always has the cholera if it exists elsewhere. We shall know in a very little while what awaits us, as " Messieurs de Santé " are just boarding the ship. Two men who probably know nothing about the proper method for such service. We of the first cabin are inspected at once, all standing in line. It is mere form, so far as we are concerned; but, following the inspectors forward, one discovers a different state of affairs. Amidships, on a raised hatchway, a Turkish family have lived for a week, the women always veiled. It has been a marvel to me how they kept so many people on that hatch without an occasional spill over; but they are spilled right and left by these inspectors. The women are unveiled and made to show their tongues, while the children are reduced to utmost woe by numerous pokes. Around about stand the ship's crew and deck passengers; and what a queer scene it is! The French faces are keen and alert, ready to make the engines go, or to sing the " Marseillaise " as they conduct us to the guillotine; the semi-intelligent faces of the Armenians, the stolid, stupid faces of the Turks, varied by one Dutch face, a Georgian or two, and one American.

Now the French crew are passing in review. Many of them, I should say, are descended from that "Vengeance," who, with Theresa Defarge, kept talley at the guillotine the day of Sidney Carton's sacrifice. A bottle of champagne to the "Messieurs de Santé," and the inspection is over. Those officers of the Star and Crescent depart with a "Bon Voyage," and we are free to do likewise. No one save the stewardess seems particularly upset by the episode. Some one suggested that she had false teeth, and "there was war in Egypt." The rest have returned to their wonted state of calm. Veiled again are the Turkish women, while that old Turk yonder has drawn over him two blankets and a comfort and gone sound asleep in the sunlight, notwithstanding that the heat must be somewhere near ninety degrees. We have one Sart on board, who seems to rest in eternal good humor and to consider life as a huge joke. Peace go with him! Allah guard his footsteps! The anchor is on its way up from the bottom, and we are

off, steaming through the gates of the Bosphorus, to stop again only in the Golden Horn.

Attractive towns crowd either bank. That
to the right, with its many villas and terraced
sides, might be Cannes or Nice, but for those
balloon-like figures in blue and red which prom-
enade the shore. Long lines of cypress trees,
so characteristic of all Turkish landscapes,
march up and down the hills, which are every
here and there crowned with ruins. The waters
are covered with sails of many colors. Between
the two great towers on the right rises a
summer hotel, built and run, I am told, by an
American. Turkey is evidently not afraid to
have her fortress overlooked, as every window
of that hotel commands a good view thereof.
On the left rise the towers of that fortress so
graphically described by General Wallace in
his " Prince of India," while further on the
Hills of Scutari block the view, and the houses
of Galata keep her company on the right, both
acting as wings for the great central picture.
Beyond the gaunt trees of " Seraglio Point,"

beyond the minarets of St. Sophia and Sultan Achmet, rises a vast jumble of roofs—rises that great desire of Russia's Czar—Stamboul.

"The Bosphorus shall be free;
It shall make room for me,
And the gates of its water-streets
Be unbarred before my fleets.
I say it: the great white Czar."

CHAPTER XXII.

STAMBOUL, and not Central Asia, is the end and aim of Russia's ambitions. She knows that she can never conquer India, and she knows that nature, in the shape of the Pamirs and the almost impassable deserts, guards her eastern possessions better than all her armies can do it. To my thinking, any war movement she makes in that direction is but a blind to cover her advance on this city of Constantine. She already controls all to the north, even if she does not own all in name; while, as the traveler passes by rail to Vienna, he will see that, like a huge cuttlefish, she has run her tentacles in to the westward; and were she not a house divided against herself, were she possessed of a government like that of Great Britain, it would not be long before St. Sophia would blaze with the jewels of the Holy Icons. We can not but wish that such might be the case, for, no matter how greatly we may disapprove of her, she is vastly better than the Turks, who, to my mind, are too nasty to be allowed to exist in Europe. But Russia is divided against herself, while state and church are surrounded by a web of intrigue only possible in an absolute monarchy. Never in the greatest days of the Church of Rome were her priests possessed of stronger temporal power than those of the Russia of to-day; and to-day all the world looks on with terror at her slowly dying emperor, the preserver of the peace of Europe, a devoted father, and an example of a faithful husband found on the thrones of Europe. Alexander the Third is dying broken-hearted, as much a victim to his form of government as is the lowest of the serfs, for they are still "serfs," though not in name. Whatever oppression has fallen on his people has come, not from himself, though all the blame will be his, but from those in office under him. They hold and sway the real authority, and in them, being Russians, is developed, by the possession of absolute power, all that brutality which lies latent in man—and it is enormous. I do not think, as he is human and not divine, that it is within the emperor's power to do away with this present order of things. Nothing save a revolution, far-reaching and bloody—a revolution one shudders to contemplate—can bring light to the darkness of "Holy Russia."

In the November days, that darkness deepens, and the end comes at Lavadia. Alexander passes before that throne that knows no difference between Czar and peasant, solves the "grand, sad subject of the immortality"; but I fancy, when the recording angel struck his name from the book of the living and entered it on the book of the dead, that he inscribed thereunder: "He hath done what he could." Peace to the soul of the Czar!

CHAPTER XXIII.

Constantinople, August 2, 1894.

LET those who possess the memory of this Ottoman capital as it was twenty years since keep that memory green and not destroy it by a visit to the city as it now exists. The change is great, and, for the lover of the picturesque, most deplorable. From the sea, Constantinople presents the same splendid appearance as of yore, and one is led to suppose that they will again see the delightful city of their memory. As you land at Pera and pass up the old familiar streets, once sacred to donkeys and sedan chairs, you notice that the latter have vanished utterly, and the former slink by as though under interdiction. Smart victorias roll along and tram-cars jingle their bells through the narrow thoroughfares. There is an inclined plane that carries one quickly to the heights above, and during the progress affords a glimpse now and then of the street of steps, down which, in the old days, you have made your stately progress in a sedan chair.

Pera is about as it used to be, save for some comfortable hotels, to which one does not object, and some blocks of fine buildings. Across from my window is a summer garden, where of old Turkish tombstones raised their stone turbans and fezes. Many of them, I notice, are being used for hitching-posts, and many of the stately cypress trees are gone forever. But the view from my window is as enchanting as of old. There, is the inner Golden Horn with its fleet of war ships; there, is the long bridge of boats to Stamboul, and beyond rise the domes and minarets of the Musselman quarter. As one descends for a visit, he notices on the bridge of boats a strange absence of color, a certain drabness that grates upon the eye; and at last discovers that the turbans and brilliant Turkish dresses of both men and women have vanished. The crowds before him are dressed in "Cheap John" English clothes, with

no jot of color save a fez now and then. Gone
are the balloon dresses of the women, vanished
are the Yashmacs, and as the carriages roll by,
the faces in them are more plainly to be seen
than in a European town. There is no shadow
of the days of old left in the costumes of the
people. I confess that it is in a disheartened
condition that I pass slowly onward. Still the
domes of St. Sophia rise over there. Surely the
old temple can not have changed with the rest.
It is useless to go "bazaarwards," as they have
been ruined by the recent earthquakes; and if
they had not, they had already lost their old-time
charm, and will never again possess it. They
will be rebuilt after some European model, and
all the old shadowy corners, with their gleam
of silver and gold, their faint odor of sandal-
wood and attar of roses, be gone forever, as
are the bevies of laughing, chattering, darkly
veiled women that were wont to follow one
around. Past the closed and ruined quarters
one goes in silence, and on and up through the
dusty streets, to what I remember as a bower of

THE RUINED BAZAARS.

beauty—the old Seraglio, a place where the cypress and myrtle mingled their fragrance with the salt of the blue waters murmuring around them—a garden of delight. Pity I had not retained my memories, but the " now " and " then " are so very different that perhaps the recollections of the latter may survive the shock of the former. The " Sublime Port " is dilapidated and dirty, and now gives entrance to a brand new government building. Through what were the shades of these gardens where of old Sultanas wandered, the Oriental Express passes, shrieking wildly; and when I ask my guide, " Where are the ruins of that marble chute down which plunged the victims of the Sultans?" he stares in wonder and points with pride to the painted railway station. What stupid fools these Turks are, to destroy that which drew thousands to their city. As Dom Pedro said of the monks of Cordova: " They have done what any one could do, but they have destroyed what was unique in the world." But enough; let us pass under the dim portals of the church of Constantine. This is as we knew it;

this is as we left it. This has escaped the destroying tooth of change and time. The very rugs, as they slant across the pavements in order to face the Holy of Holies, bring back each and every face to my memory which I saw when I trod them years ago, while the silence and sacredness of the old temple penetrates and calms one's soul. Through the dim light flutter stray pigeons, and from the base of a column which once supported the temple of Diana at Ephesus, comes the droning voice of an old Turk. He wears his green turban, and he is reciting the Koran for the benefit of his soul. Over all soars the marvelous dome, and off in an eastern nook, still to be seen, though more faintly now than of yore, is the outline of the Virgin's figure, lasting through all these centuries, and being the only semblance of the human form to be found in St. Sophia. After all, there is but one St. Sophia, and no other temple on earth approaches it for impressiveness. Under its arches you will linger long, from its portals you will depart with regret; and wherever your footsteps may lead you in life's journey, you will carry with you always a remembrance of its deep peace, its benediction of repose to soul and body. All the Christian world must sympathize with the desires of the Greek Church to possess again this "Mecca" of her faith, to sweep forever from St. Sophia the taint of Mohammed, to raise aloft the cross of Christ after its banishment of a thousand years, to unveil forever more the face of the mother of God.

> "And the Christian shall no more
> Be crushed, as heretofore,
> Beneath thine iron rule,
> O Sultan of Istamboul!
> I swear it! I, the Czar,
> Batyushka: Gosudar!" *

FINIS.

* *"Father-dear, sovereign."*